She'd gone to Paradise and found hell...

Now she'd gone to Texas and found Damien. The first had ruined her life and left her an emotional wreck. The second was likely to break her heart.

She was not what the cowboy needed, and he'd realize that as soon as he was through saving her.

She pulled out her pajamas from the travel case. Then, unable to help herself, she reached for the silky chemise inside. She held it in front of her in the full-length mirror.

She hardly recognized the woman staring back at her—the Emma she used to be.

Damien knocked on the door she'd left ajar. "How about a nightcap to—"

She saw his face reflected in the mirror. The chemise pooled to the floor, leaving her feeling exposed, though she was still dressed.

A second later Damien wrapped his arms around her from behind.

She turned and with tears she could neither explain nor stop, she lifted her mouth to his and melted in his kiss.

JOANNA WAYNE

SON OF A GUN

™ Harlequin®

TORONTO NEW YORK LONDON
AMSTERDAM PARIS SYDNEY HAMBURG
STOCKHOLM ATHENS TOKYO MILAN MADRID
PRAGUE WARSAW BUDAPEST AUCKLAND

Thanks to Dr. Lindsey Whitehurst for her information on how a veterinarian might help out in an emergency. A special thanks to all my psychology professors who taught me so much about abnormal behavior, though of course I took liberties with their lectures. And thanks to my husband for putting up with me when deadlines make me a pain to live with.

Recycling programs
for this product may
not exist in your area.

ISBN-13: 978-0-373-69608-6

SON OF A GUN

Copyright © 2012 by Jo Ann Vest

Printed in U.S.A.

ABOUT THE AUTHOR

Joanna Wayne was born and raised in Shreveport, Louisiana, and received her undergraduate and graduate degrees from LSU-Shreveport. She moved to New Orleans in 1984, and it was there that she attended her first writing class and joined her first professional writing organization. Her debut novel, *Deep in the Bayou*, was published in 1994.

Now, dozens of published books later, Joanna has made a name for herself as being on the cutting edge of romantic suspense in both series and single-title novels. She has been on the Waldenbooks bestseller list for romance and has won many industry awards. She is also a popular speaker at writing organizations and local community functions and has taught creative writing at the University of New Orleans Metropolitan College.

Joanna currently resides in a small community forty miles north of Houston, Texas, with her husband. Though she still has many family and emotional ties to Louisiana, she loves living in the Lone Star State. You may write Joanna at P.O. Box 852, Montgomery, Texas 77356.

Books by Joanna Wayne

HARLEQUIN INTRIGUE

*Four Brothers of Colts Run Cross
‡Special Ops Texas
†Sons of Troy Ledger
**Big "D" Dads

CAST OF CHARACTERS

Emma Muran—aka Emma Smith. She is on the run from a kidnapper who cannot afford to let her go free.

Damien Lambert—He's the oldest son of a powerful and influential Texas business and ranching family.

Tague and Durk Lambert—Damien's brothers. Durk is involved in the family oil business. Tague manages and works the ranch with Damien.

Carolina Lambert—Damien's mother, who is still grieving for her husband, Hugh, who died a few months ago.

Sheriff Walter Garcia—Local sheriff.

Julio—Operates a human trafficking operation.

Caudillo—Wealthy arms dealer who lures women to his private island in the Caribbean and holds them captive.

Grandma Pearl—Damien's grandmother. She can be a bit mischievous at times.

Aunt Sybil—Damien's aunt who lives on the Bent Pine Ranch with the rest of the Lambert family.

Blake Benson—A veterinarian who owns the ranch next to the Lamberts and helps out in an emergency.

Dorothy Paul—Emma's friend who was supposed to go with her on vacation.

Carson Stile—A good friend of Damien's, an expert tech guy who never reveals how he gets his information from the internet.

Chale—Caudillo's head guard.

Prologue

Damien Lambert worked the curry comb in a circular motion, talking to King as he did. The black steed stood contentedly even though thunder growled continuously and zigzagging bolts of lightning split the sky, the glaring streaks of light visible through the open barn doors.

The other horses in the barn were also calmed by Damien's soothing voice and company. Only Jolie, his mother's pale gray quarter horse, pawed the hay-covered dirt as if she knew something about the approaching storm they didn't.

Normally, Damien appreciated a good thunderstorm. It watered the pastures and refilled the creeks. The fierceness even had a way of clearing the air, a release of the occasional friction that erupted between him and his father. At times the two locked horns so tightly that Damien didn't see how they could keep working together in the same state, much less on the same ranch.

Hugh Lambert. Bigger than life. A man who swore like a sailor, liked his bourbon a little too much at times and who'd go up against any politician with rhetoric, clout and his considerable wealth if he thought their policies interfered with him running his spread or his oil company as he saw fit.

But Hugh was also a man who'd fire his best wrangler or even a foreman in a second if he found they'd mistreated an animal. And even in the business world, he was a man whose word and handshake were as binding as a contract.

Damien had grown to appreciate that more and more as he'd matured. And when his father wasn't reaming him out, Damien realized how lucky he was to have Hugh as a father. It had made him the man he was. Independent, tough and thick-skinned.

A clap of thunder fired like an explosion. Apprehension surfaced and weighed on Damien's mind. His father and some of his ranching buddies had flown by private jet to the Cowboys/Cardinals game in Arizona. That would put their return flight straight in the path of the storm.

But they'd run into weather like this enough times that they knew the risk. When the weather warranted, the pilot landed the plane in any small airport in their path or else postponed the trip home until the next day.

Damien finished currying King and was brushing him down when he heard his brother Tague yelling for him. By the time Damien reached the barn door, Tague was standing there, out of breath, panic rolling off him like the dust the wind had kicked up.

"It's Dad." Tague's words were shaky and barely audible.

Anxiety pitted in Damien's stomach. "What happened?"

"The plane crashed." Tague slumped against the door.

"Where?"

"Somewhere in West Texas."

Damien felt something crack inside him, and he held on to a post for support. "How did you find out?"

"Sheriff Garcia is at the house. Dad's dead, Damien." Panic tore at Tague's voice. "Mother's just standing there.

She's not even crying, but her eyes…they look like she's dying, too."

Adrenaline bucked off the paralyzing shock. Damien took off running. He thought he heard Tague's footsteps behind him, but he didn't slow down or wait for his youngest brother. His dad couldn't be dead. This was all some horrible mistake. They'd find that out later, but his mother needed Damien now.

Chapter One

Three Months Later

The truck rocked and bounced along what felt like a dry, stony creek bed. Emma Muran's stomach rolled violently as she was jostled and pressed against the sweaty bodies that were crammed into the back of the type of small rental trailer used for moving furniture. Only this one was painted a dull gray.

Though the air outside was bitter cold, the air inside the crowded trailer was stagnant, the odors of urine and perspiration sickening. Babies cried. A kid in the back was begging to go home. An old woman wailed and murmured heart-wrenching prayers as she clung to her rosary beads.

The woman next to Emma slumped against her as her baby pushed away from the woman's semi-bared breast and began to cry again.

"Would you like me to hold him for a few minutes?" Emma offered, avoiding looking directly at her. Making eye contact created a bond. Emma couldn't afford a bond, no matter how tenuous.

"She's a girl," the young mother said, pulling away the lightweight cotton scarf she'd been using as a privacy shield so that Emma could see the baby's delicate white dress and tiny yellow trimmed booties. "She's eight weeks old. Her name is Belle."

The woman's voice was weak, her eyes wet and filmy as if covered with transparent gauze.

"She's beautiful," Emma said, "and the dress is exquisite."

"I made it myself for when she sees her papa in Dallas for the first time. I saved as much as I could from every dollar he sent us to live on until I had enough to pay for this trip."

"Why does she keep crying? Is she sick?"

"She's hungry."

"You just fed her."

"I don't have enough milk to satisfy her."

"Didn't you bring a bottle of formula to supplement?"

"Ningún dinero."

No money. No doubt she'd spent every cent she could scrape up to get to her baby's father. Emma had paid three thousand American dollars to be treated like cattle.

"Does your husband know you're coming?" Emma asked.

She shook her head. "No married, but Juan Perez is a good man. He take care of us in Texas." Emma assumed the woman wasn't an American citizen. Why else would she pay to be smuggled into the country? Emma was likely the only citizen amidst this group of desperate elderly people and mothers with children.

Yet she was no less desperate. Her fate in Mexico was certain death. And in America, as well, if the monster found her.

The baby started to cry louder. Poor thing. Emma weighed her own terrifying fears against the baby's needs. Staying unnoticed was no longer an option.

"This baby is hungry," Emma called in Spanish over

the clattering rattles of the truck. "If you can spare a few sips of milk. Please."

Finally, a young mother whom Emma had noticed earlier nursing a boy of about six months reached for the baby without a word. A stranger's hands took Belle and passed the crying infant to the woman. Exhausted from crying, Belle sucked for only a few minutes before falling asleep.

By this time, Belle's frail mother had slumped against the shoulder of the young man next to her and seemed to have fallen into a deep sleep. Emma took the dozing infant and cuddled her to her own chest.

So precious. So innocent. She hadn't asked for any of this.

The truck came to a jerking stop and bodies collided with each other like rotting melons. The back door opened and everyone gasped as if choking on the fresh air their lungs craved.

The man in charge, who they knew only as Julio, climbed aboard. "We crossed the border a few miles back. You're in Texas."

A cheer went up from the disheveled group.

Tears wet Emma's eyes. She was back on American soil. A week ago, she'd all but given up hope of that ever happening. Unfortunately, even here she'd have to find a way to change her identity so completely that Emma Muran ceased to exist.

"If you want out now, you're welcome to haul ass and take off on your own," Julio continued. "But you're pretty much in the middle of nowhere. I'll take you all the way to Dallas if you stay on board, just as promised when you paid and signed on."

About half of the trailer's occupants pushed and shoved their way to the door. They knew that the longer they stayed on the truck the more chance they'd have of being stopped by border patrol or other law-enforcement officers and returned to Mexico.

For the most part, the ones who stayed seated had young children with them or were so frail they would have had difficulty making the trek across rough terrain on a freezing night. Even in January, bitter cold like this was extremely rare in South Texas.

Emma considered her options and decided to bolt, though she had no idea where she was. If she was arrested, the agents would immediately recognize that she was an American. She'd be forced to try to explain why a citizen was sneaking back into the country in a despicable human-trafficking operation.

She'd be fingerprinted and identified. And then there would be no avoiding the media blitz that would surround her return. Caudillo would instantly have a hundred men on her trail, and no amount of security could protect her.

The baby stirred in Emma's arms. She turned to hand Belle back to the mother, but the woman had been shoved to the middle of the trailer, facedown, her arms and legs askew, as if she were a rag doll who'd been dropped and left to lie as she fell.

"What's the matter with that one?" Julio asked.

Several who'd stayed behind shrugged and shook their heads. Julio climbed into the trailer and turned the young mother over so that she stared at the ceiling with blank, lifeless eyes. "Anybody here with her?"

Emma was about to answer that she was holding the woman's baby, but a warning stare from the mother who'd nursed the baby silenced her.

"No use to transport the dead." Julio picked up the body and tossed it off the back of the trailer. "Anyone else feeling sickly?" He smirked at his sick joke.

Belle started to fuss.

Julio turned and stared at Emma as if seeing her for the first time. He leered openly and then smiled as if they shared some private joke. Did he know that the baby in her arms was not hers?

Emma quieted Belle with a gentle rocking movement and avoided eye contact with Julio.

Julio took the gun from the holster at his waist and waved it around, asserting his authority. "The rest of you have five minutes to relieve yourself and stretch. You'll get food as you climb back into your smelly nests."

The woman who'd nursed Belle motioned for Emma to follow her into a dense thicket of shrubs, the best they could find in the way of privacy. They took turns holding the babies while the other relieved herself. Emma took her last packaged hand wipe from her pocket, tore it in half and shared it with the woman.

"What will you do with the baby?" the woman asked in Spanish.

"I don't know." The enormity of the problem she'd just taken on hit her full force.

"Julio will toss her out like rubbish if he finds out she belongs to the dead woman."

"But what am I supposed to do with her?"

Suspicion darkened the woman's eyes. "American?"

Emma shook her head and then shuddered and pulled her colorful rebozo low over her forehead so that only the bangs of her horrid wig showed as she approached the trailer.

Emma had counted on her clothing, the wig and her proficiency with the Spanish language to help her pass for a Mexican national. Otherwise, they would have thought she was an undercover cop or an investigative reporter. Either would have gotten her kicked out.

Julio passed out bottles of water and tortillas filled with

bean paste as they reached the truck. Emma took only the water. She had a pocketful of wrapped churros and tortillas she'd bought in the small village where they'd begun their journey. Those would hold her over until she could get to Dallas.

Her other purchases had been made in the city where her escape boat docked. Her first purchase had been the wiry black wig she was wearing. In the same department store, she'd purchased the long colorful skirt, a Mexican-style white shirt, a bra, panties and basic hygiene items.

She'd quickly changed out of the long silk dress she'd been wearing when she escaped the monster. The better she blended in with the populations in the small villages she'd be traveling through, the better her chances of staying alive.

She'd bought the handmade rebozo at the last village for the explicit purpose of covering her head so that little of the wig could be seen beneath the bunched cotton shawl. It was the only protection she had now from the icy wind.

Julio grabbed her arm as she scrambled back into the trailer, forcing her to face him for a few seconds before he released his grip. His leering, lustful stare made her skin crawl.

"Guess we're ready to roll," Julio said. He jumped off the back of the trailer and slammed the doors shut.

Minutes later, the engine sputtered back to life and the jerky, bumpy ride began again. Only now Emma held the baby of a dead woman in her arms. How in the world did she ever expect to take care of a helpless infant when she was on the run?

Belle squirmed and balled her tiny hands into fists, swinging them into the air and twisting her lips into a pitiful pout. Emma trailed a finger down the baby's smooth cheek. Belle seemed soothed by the touch.

A quivery sensation stirred deep inside Emma, as if Belle had latched herself to Emma's heart.

WOOD SMOKE CURLED FROM the chimney and filled Damien's nostrils as he stamped the mud from his feet and climbed onto the back porch of the sprawling ranch house. His brother Durk appeared before he reached the door, carrying an armload of firewood from the nearby shed. Damien held the door for him.

"I wondered when you'd give it up and get out of that sleet," Durk said.

"Had to move cattle into one of the closer pastures in case that snow they're promising actually develops."

"Don't you have wranglers for that?"

"I had them all working most of the day, too. This is a ranch, not that plush suite of offices you work in, bro."

"Don't think I don't know it. Cows are much easier to deal with than corporate policy and endless regulations."

Durk was the CEO of Lambert Inc, and spent only his weekends at the ranch. But Damien didn't let up on him. "Don't worry, if it snows tonight, you'll be recruited for ranch-hand duty in the morning," he said. "When did you get here?"

"About an hour ago. I would have been here sooner, but there was a major traffic jam coming out of Dallas. Bridges and overpasses are already icing over. Not a fit night out for man nor beast, with the exception of polar bears—and there's not a lot of them wondering around North Texas."

"It's awful quiet around here. Where is everybody?"

"Grandma's back in her suite. Aunt Sybil is in her room watching TV and sipping her afternoon sherry. And Tague is chauffeuring Mother. I told him to be careful driving in this."

"Where did they go?"

"Just over to the Double R."

"In this weather? Whatever for?"

"To take Mildred and Hank Ross some of the beef-and-vegetable soup she made this afternoon. Apparently Mildred's been sick, and you know Mother. She thinks she has to look out for the whole county."

"When did they leave?"

"Just after I arrived, but they were going to stop off and try to persuade Karen Legasse to come stay with us until the weather improves."

"That would make for an interesting weekend," Damien said. "You and your ex-girlfriend snowed in together."

"*Ex* is the operative word there," Durk said. "She's married now, with a baby. No way am I going near that, even if the sparks hadn't cooled to ice."

"It may be over between you two," Damien said, "but she and Mother are closer than ever. Karen shows up at the Bent Pine almost as often as the mailman."

Damien went to the coffeepot and filled a mug with the hot brew. "Where is Mark the Magnificent?"

"Apparently dear hubby is in L.A. for a meeting."

"And missing all the poopy diapers. Those rich investment types know how to suffer."

Damien lifted the lid off the big pot on the back burner of the range. The heady aroma of onions, stewed tomatoes and spices filled the room. His stomach rumbled in anticipation of his mother's famous homemade soup.

"I'm going to grab a quick shower," Damien said, "unless you need help bringing in logs." With three fireplaces in the rambling old house—they could burn a lot of wood on a cold weekend.

"I've got it covered," Durk said. "And then I'll get to those boxes in the attic Mother asked me to bring down."

"The attic is full of boxes. Did she say which ones she wants?"

"Yeah. The ones she scooted next to the opening."

"I'll get started on the boxes," Damien said. "The shower can wait a few more minutes."

Not that he liked the idea of his mother spending another long weekend buried in grief and memories. Since his father's death, she'd spent far too much time going through old chests, boxes and trunks. It was as if she were trying to hold on to him by reliving every moment of their past.

Damien had no need for pictures or mementos. His father was so much a part of the ranch that he felt his presence every minute of the day. That didn't lessen his pain or the regret that he'd never had a chance to tell his dad how much he loved and appreciated him. The two of them had tended to leave too many good things unsaid.

He finished his coffee, deposited the cup on the counter and took the stairs to the second floor. Once in the hallway, he reached for the overhead grip and pulled down the ladder. He climbed quickly to the dusty attic. Dusk was closing in fast, and he switched on the light to dispel the shadows.

His mother had four cardboard boxes and one sturdy metal file box that resembled an old-fashioned safe piled near the rectangular opening. He'd never noticed the metal safe in the attic before.

He scanned the area and realized that the large black trunk in the back corner was standing open. That trunk had been padlocked for as long as he could remember.

In fact, once when he and Durk were kids and had been playing hide-and-seek in the attic, they'd made up a horror tale about a body being buried in that banged-up old trunk.

His curiosity piqued again, Damien walked over to

the trunk. One side of it was empty, a space easily large enough to have accommodated the metal safe.

The rest of the trunk held a half dozen or so old photo albums. He picked one up and opened the tattered cover. He didn't recognize anyone in the picture, but one of the men was definitely a Lambert, an older version of Hugh.

One of the photos had fallen loose from the old-fashioned black tabs that had held it in place. Damien turned it over and read the names of the people in the picture. The man in work coveralls was Damien's great-great-grandfather, Oliver Lambert, the original owner of the Bent Pine Ranch.

Hugh had made sure Damien and his brothers knew all about the blood, sweat, tears and glory that had gone into building this ranch. The man standing beside Oliver was Damien's great-grandfather as a young man.

Damien picked up a new photo album, this one not quite as old. He slipped one of the pictures from its tabs. Again the names were written on the back of the photo.

Damien's great-grandfather was standing beside a magnificent black stallion. The boy in the saddle was Damien's grandfather. The house in the background was the same as the one Damien was in right now, although several wings had been added over the years.

Alive and dead, the Lambert roots extended deep into the earth of Bent Pine Ranch. His ancestors were buried in a cemetery near the chapel that Damien's great-great-grandfather had built for his own wedding. All the succeeding Lambert weddings, including Damien's parents', had been solemnized in that same small, weathered chapel.

If Damien ever married, he'd hopefully continue the tradition. The "if" loomed larger every day. Not that Damien hadn't dated. He'd just never clicked with a woman the way he figured a guy should click with someone he intended to spend the rest of his life with.

Damien closed the trunk but didn't bother to latch the padlock. He made quick work of delivering the boxes to his mother's bedroom.

That done, he made a last trip up the ladder, picked up the portable safe and muttered a curse as the lid fell open. Files and loose papers scattered about the floor, a few floating through the attic opening to the hallway below. He stared for a few seconds, tempted to leave the mess until tomorrow. It wasn't like his mother would get to all the boxes tonight.

But his father had taught him too well. If a job needed doing, do it right and do it now.

Damien stooped to his haunches and began to gather the scattered papers. There were baptismal records, old report cards, outdated contracts and files containing yellowed documents. He checked the date on a receipt for fifty head of cattle. He'd paid more than that for the last bull he'd purchased at auction.

The receipt was dated thirty-one years ago, thirteen months before he was born. He figured the old records would make interesting reading over a cold weekend.

Working quickly, he gathered the loose papers by the handful and slid them into the box without putting them in any kind of order or attempting to return them to the correct files. He paused when an old birth certificate caught his eye.

The name of the baby boy was Damien Briggs, almost identical to his name, except that he was Damien Briggs Lambert. Briggs was his mother's maiden name.

The date of birth was exactly the same as his. He found that uncannily weird. He kept reading.

The mother was listed as Melissa Briggs. The father

was unnamed. The Melissa in question must have been his mother's sister. His mother seldom talked about her family, but she had mentioned a sister named Melissa who'd died years ago.

Somehow Damien had gotten the impression that Melissa had died when she was only a child, but apparently not so if she'd given birth to a boy on the same day he'd been born.

So where was this first cousin that Damien had never heard mentioned? Had he died in the accident that had also killed his mother?

Damien read the names and dates again. Disturbing possibilities surfaced. Was it possible that he and Damien Briggs were one and the same? Could it be that his real mother was Melissa Briggs?

No. Carolina was his mother. Hugh was his father. He'd seen his own birth certificate.

Still, the troubling suspicions refused to dislodge themselves from his mind. Acquiring a fake birth certificate listing himself as the father would have been no sweat at all for a man with the political clout of Hugh Lambert.

But then again, Hugh would never give his name to a son who wasn't his. Case closed.

His mother's voice drifted from the kitchen. She was home. Damien should just confront her with the birth certificate. She'd clear up the confusion. It would be over and done with.

But if his suspicions were on target, it would explain why Hugh had frequently treated him like a wild horse that he'd captured but didn't really want in his fold.

More disturbed than he was willing to admit, Damien carried the safe downstairs and left it sitting on the coffee table. He marched out the front door, pulling it shut tight behind him.

Flakes of snow fell on his shirt and in his hair. A frigid cold settled in his bones, but he didn't go back for his jacket. Instead, he walked toward the horse barn.

He needed to be alone to think. He needed to escape the confines of the house and to ride the open spaces of a ranch that might not really be his legacy at all.

Chapter Two

The truck jerked to a stop. Bodies squirmed and stretched. Belle balled her tiny hands into fists and swung them in the air as if she sensed the excitement growing around her.

The back doors squeaked open and a welcoming burst of fresh but frigid air filled Emma's lungs. The darkness of night had set in completely since their last stop. She cuddled Belle closer inside the folds of her rebozo.

"El fin de la línea," Julio called.

The end of the line. They'd made it safely.

An elderly man near the door stuck his head out and then frowned. "No Dallas."

"Esto es Dallas, *anciano,"* Julio insisted.

But they were clearly not in the city. Others began to voice their fears.

"Estamos en Dallas?"

"Espero que no sea probemas."

"Tonto," Julio quipped. "If I let you out in the middle of town, you'd be arrested in minutes. You can see the highway from here," he shouted over their complaints. "Catch a ride into town or walk. You'll be in the outskirts of Dallas in less than a mile."

Emma didn't complain. If he was telling the truth, she could make that even carrying Belle. As soon as she came to a convenience store, she'd call for a cab and have it take her to the nearest cheap motel.

The grumbling and curses continued, making it clear that the occupants didn't trust Julio. Not that they could do anything about it.

Emma placed Belle on her lap while she gathered her rebozo and wound it around her as she'd seen other mothers do, knotting it into a sling so that it would keep Belle cuddled against her chest and leave both hands free as she climbed from the trailer.

The woman who'd befriended her and fed Belle pushed a plastic bag holding a pacifier into Emma's hand. "This one is sterile. To comfort the infant until you find milk."

"Gracias." Emma slipped the wrapped pacifier into the deep layered folds of her wrap and reached for the paper bag that held her new purchases.

Julio grabbed Emma's arm when she reached the door and yanked her back into the trailer. "You stay."

Her stomach rolled. Not this. Not again. "The baby," she whispered, as if that would make a difference to this beast.

He shoved her against the wall. "Do as I say or you won't be getting out of here alive."

One of the men looked back, shame in his eyes that he didn't have the strength or the courage to stand up for her. She avoided meeting his gaze, not wanting him to get shot on her account.

Dread ebbed through her veins. Would she never be free?

Once the trailer was empty except for her and Belle, Julio shoved her against the wall and slammed the double doors shut. A few minutes later, they were bouncing along again, litter left by the former occupants rolling and scratching along the floor.

Emma's body was jerked around like a marionette, and she struggled to make certain it was just her shoulders and elbows that banged into the side of the trailer and not Belle's head.

Belle began to cry and Emma offered her the pacifier. The baby continued to wail, fighting the nipple. Eventually she locked her lips around it and stopped fretting.

Emma fought the growing panic as the truck rumbled along. The thought of rape made her violently ill. But how could she fight him off? Julio was twice her size and carrying a weapon.

Had she escaped ten months of captivity only to be raped and killed by some half-drunk thug on a deserted road? And if she was, what would happen to Belle?

The answer to that was too heartbreaking to consider. Emma would have to find a way to save them.

Unfortunately, no miraculous ideas came to mind.

Belle was sleeping when the truck bolted and then jerked to a stop. Emma's heart jumped to her throat when the doors clanked and rattled open. She jumped up as Julio climbed inside, the illumination from his flashlight in the confines of the trailer casting a demonlike glow about his face.

An owl hooted in the distance. The wind whistled through the tops of trees. But there were no highway sounds. No lights behind him. No sign of anyone to hear if she screamed for help.

Julio moved toward her, the smell of whiskey strong on his fetid breath. "Put the baby on the floor," he demanded, "and then lie down on your back."

"You don't want to do this," she said.

"Sure I do, *mujerzuela.*"

She shook her head at the cruel taunt. "I'm not a slut. Please, I'm a mother. Let me be. I paid my money."

"I'll let you be when I'm done with you. Do as I say and I won't hurt you or the baby. Cause trouble and you both die here. Now, put the baby down and spread your legs."

It was foolish to try to fight him. It would get her hurt or killed. Then the monster Caudillo would have won without even being here.

She was still standing when Julio put his hand beneath her skirt and trailed his hand along her thigh, inching closer to her intimate areas. Emma's insides rebelled and her instincts took over. Her knee flew up and caught him in the crotch. He yelped and staggered backward. She swung at him and her fingernails dug into the flesh below his left eye, leaving two bloody trails.

He muttered curses and recovered his balance, slapping her so hard her brain seemed to rattle in her skull. Belle began to wail. If Emma didn't stop now, the baby would surely get hurt.

She was about to give in when she spotted the sharp blade of a knife he grasped with his right hand.

"Please, no. The baby needs me."

He spit in her direction, the spittle falling short and landing near her feet. "Should I cut your pretty throat or just shred your face so that you never tempt another man again?"

"Please. Mercy. Please."

He dabbed at the blood on his face with the dirty cuff of his sleeve and then swung at her. The knife slashed her left arm a few inches above the elbow, barely missing Belle.

Julio swung again, but this time he missed completely and lost his balance when the blade connected with nothing but air.

Bracing herself with her left arm against the side of the trailer, she got in a quick kick that struck him in the back of the knee. He fell facedown onto the hard, filthy floor.

Emma scurried to jump out the back door. Expecting to hear Julio's footsteps behind her or the sound of a gunshot, she didn't look back until she reached the cover of trees and brush at the side of the narrow dirt road where they were parked. To her amazement, there was no sign of Julio.

She shuddered at the icy sting of the wind in her face and the feel of warm blood running down her arm. Working quickly, she tightened the rebozo around the wound, hoping the pressure would slow the bleeding.

Belle started to cry. Emma fought back her own tears of fear and frustration. She had had no idea which way she should go, but she stumbled ahead, vaguely aware of the snowflakes sifting through the canopy of pine needles and melting against her cheeks. She wrapped her arms around Belle and held her close in a futile effort to keep her warm.

Finally, she stepped into a clearing and spied a stretch of barbed-wire fencing. Relief pumped a reviving surge of adrenaline though her veins. If there was a fence, civilization couldn't be that far away. Her pace quickened with her pulse.

Careful not to let the barbs touch Belle's tender skin, Emma stretched the top wire so that she could maneuver through the fence and step into the tree-dotted pasture.

Something rustled in the grass behind her, and Emma took off running, terrified that Julio might be mere steps behind her. She didn't stop running until she was panting for breath and her legs felt like they were about to give way and send her slamming to the ground.

Her heart still pounding, she fell against the trunk of a towering pine tree. Belle began to fret, and her fussing quickly escalated to a wail.

With her back against the scratchy bark of the tree trunk, Emma slowly sank to the ground. Her fingers searched and found the pacifier nestled in the deep folds of her rebozo. She poked the nipple into Belle's mouth. This time Belled quickly locked her lips around it. But in in a few short minutes, she spit it out.

Belle began to wail again. Emma closed her eyes and pictured herself in a comfortable rocker, cuddling Belle while the hungry infant fed on nourishing formula. Heat from logs blazing in a stone fireplace warmed them both, so real she could smell the odor of burning wood.

The sound of galloping hooves penetrated her consciousness. She opened her eyes and jerked to attention, but there was no horse in sight.

Like the fire and the rocker, it was only her imagination. No one would be out riding after dark on a night like this. No hero was going to come to her rescue.

She forced herself back to her feet. If she fell asleep with only illusions of comfort, the helpless infant in her arms might die before morning from the cold if not from hunger.

THE WIND WAS PUNISHING even though the old leather work jacket Damien had taken from the tack room protected him from the worst of the cold.

He'd ridden hard, letting King go full speed across the familiar trails just the way the steed loved it. Fortunately, the ride had given Damien a chance to lower his aggravation level and ease his suspicions.

This wasn't like the disagreements he used to have with his dad. Riding hard wouldn't negate the questions. The answers would have to come from his mother. No doubt she'd be able to explain everything. And most likely he'd overreacted and none of it would have anything to do with him.

Sisters might easily decide to give their sons identical

names if they'd given birth on the exact same day. One thing he knew for certain: his mother would never have willingly shut her sister's son out of her life. Either that son was dead or his father had kept Carolina away from her nephew.

Unless Damien's mother harbored family secrets so terrifying and depraved that she'd kept them hidden all these years....

The thought of his mother with deep, dark secrets was so inconceivable it was almost laughable. Honesty was practically synonymous with the name Carolina Lambert in their part of their country. So was charity and friendship.

The snow fell harder, huge flakes that were beginning to cover the winter feed grass. In some parts of the country, the first snowfall of the season was a rite of passage into winter. In Dallas, they sometimes went years without a decent snowfall. This one just might be it, though it wouldn't stay on the ground long. Warmer weather was forecasted to arrive in a couple of days.

He turned King back toward the ranch, letting him choose his own pace, until Damien spotted a young buck drinking from Beaver Creek. He reined in King and admired the stately deer. It looked totally at ease with the weather, though the wind wailed through the pine needles like a tomcat. Or like a baby.

Too much like a baby.

Damien's senses sharpened. He stretched in the saddle and spotted a woman, her shoulders stooped, trudging along in the opposite direction. He quickly caught up with her. When she turned around, he noticed that all she had for warmth was a shawl wrapped around her and the wailing infant she cuddled close to her chest.

What the devil was she doing out here with a baby on

a night like this? Damien scanned the area for trouble as he climbed from the saddle.

"Are you alone?" he asked as he shed his jacket.

She nodded. "Yes, but please don't hurt me."

Fear bled into her pleading voice. The accent was clearly American and Southern. "I have no intention of hurting you. How did you get here?"

"I…I ran my car into a ditch. I saw the fence and hoped there was a house nearby where I could find shelter. The baby is cold."

"There's no highway out here."

"There is a road," she protested. "I just left it."

"An old logging road, but no one drives on that in a car. It's full of ruts and dangerous potholes."

"I know that now. But it was dark when I turned onto it and I mistook it for a driveway."

He slipped his jacket over her shoulders.

It practically swallowed her. He was six feet tall and broad shouldered. She was a good six or seven inches shorter and petite. The jacket would keep her and the baby both warm until he could get her out of the weather.

She winced as he tugged the jacket tighter. He looked down and spotted the crimson stain on her wrap.

"You're injured."

"It's nothing, just a scratch."

But it had bled too much to be a mere scratch. Her story of the ditched car sounded more suspect by the minute. "Are you sure someone didn't dump you out here?"

"I told you, I lost control of my car and now it's stuck in a muddy ditch. I must have caught my arm on the fence when I climbed through the strings of barbed wire."

She turned away, clearly not wanting to say more. He wouldn't push the issue yet.

"Here, let me help you onto the horse. You and the baby

can ride. I'll keep the reins and walk beside you. We don't have far to go."

"Where are you taking us?"

"To a roaring fire where you and the baby can get warm. What is it anyway, a boy or a girl?"

"A girl. Her name is Belle." She looked around. "Where am I?"

"On Bent Pine Ranch."

"In Dallas?"

"Actually, you're in a tiny community known as Oak Grove, but Dallas is the closest city."

"How far are we from the city limits?"

"About twenty miles as the crow flies. Thirty miles if you're not flapping your wings. Where were you going anyway?"

"To visit my aunt, but I must have made a wrong turn somewhere."

"Maybe several. Where does she live?"

"On the outskirts of Dallas."

"That covers a lot of territory."

He helped the woman into the saddle and then zipped the jacket with both her and the baby inside the cocoon of warmth. "My name's Damien," he said, once they started toward the ranch house.

"I'm Emma."

"Do you have a last name?"

She hesitated a tad too long to be believable.

"Smith… Emma Smith."

That beat Jane Doe, but not by much. The swaying rhythm of King's walk seemed to calm the baby. In minutes, she stopped crying altogether.

Questions about his own past withdrew to the back corners of Damien's mind as the focus of his attention shifted to the more immediate concern of aiding the mystery woman and child.

He didn't fully buy the ditched-car story, though he couldn't come up with any more logical reason for her to be out in his pasture on a night like this.

It didn't matter at this point. The woman and the baby needed help. Even if she was lying, he had no choice but to take them home with him.

EMMA STUDIED THE COWBOY walking beside her. He was ruggedly handsome, with a chiseled jawline, a classic nose and hair that jutted out over his forehead from beneath a worn Western hat. Masculine. Virile.

Protective. She'd never appreciated that quality in a man more than she did right now.

Hopefully he wasn't the overly inquisitive kind. If he did ask questions, she'd have no choice but to elaborate on her original lie. If she told the truth, he'd call the cops.

Not that she wouldn't like to sic the law on Julio, but publicity of any kind would make it that much easier for Caudillo to find her.

"You picked a bad night for traveling," Damien said. "The bridges and overpasses are all slick and icy."

"I didn't expect it to turn this bad when I left home." That was the understatement of a lifetime. She'd left last March, expecting a week in paradise. She'd gotten ten months in hell.

"Where are you from?" Damien asked.

"Originally or now?"

"Now."

"Victoria, Texas." Another lie, but she'd heard someone in the trailer mention it and she knew it was south of Houston.

"Where are you from originally?"

"Nashville," she said, this time answering truthfully. She hadn't lived there since...since the last major upheaval in her life.

The smell of burning wood grew stronger. She hadn't imagined it earlier. A few minutes later, she caught her first glimpse of smoke rising from three chimneys that accentuated the steep lines of a multi-gabled roof.

The house was two-storied and sprawled out in several directions, as if it had stretched over the open land like creeping phlox.

"Who owns the ranch?" she asked as they drew nearer.

"The Lamberts."

He surely wasn't a Lambert, not wearing the tattered leather jacket he'd lent her. More likely he was just a working cowboy. "Where do you live?"

"You're looking at it."

That surprised her. "Do you and your wife have children?"

"Nope. No children. No wife, either."

"So, how many people live in the house?"

"Six when we're all present and accounted for."

"That sounds like a houseful."

"Always room for one more."

"I won't be staying," she said quickly. "I'll get out of your hair as soon as I can get a ride to the nearest motel. Any will do."

"You're nowhere near a motel, and you'd be hard-pressed to find transportation into town tonight. Even if you could, I wouldn't recommend it. You might end up worse than merely in a ditch. Besides, there's plenty of room here."

As they approached the house, she was even more awed by its sheer size. But that wasn't all it had going for it.

A large glass-enclosed porch extended across part of

the back of the house. The lamps were turned on and their soft glow fell across sofas, rockers, hooked rugs, potted plants and baskets in all shapes and sizes. A round table in the middle of the room held a huge winter arrangement of greenery, berries and cones.

To the left of that was a covered entryway that led into the house, and to the left of that were wide, uncovered windows that opened into a massive kitchen filled with people. Evidently, they were enjoying a late dinner.

Damien stopped at the base of a winter-bare oak near the back of the house. He took the reins and looped them over a low branch, securing the horse before reaching to help Emma dismount.

Anxiety swelled inside her. There would surely be questions. They'd know she was lying. They might just call the sheriff and have him come pick her up. All it would take was a fingerprint check and then there would be no hiding from the glare of the media.

Woman Kidnapped While Vacationing in the Caribbean Islands Escapes, the headline would read.

No one escaped Caudillo and lived to tell about it.

Damien's touch was firm but gentle. "Relax," he said, obviously sensing her nervousness. "The Lamberts can be a cantankerous bunch, but they don't bite. You're safe."

Safe. Even the sound of the word made her breath catch. But the safety Damien or the Lamberts could provide was only temporary, little more than an illusion.

SURPRISINGLY, THE ANXIETY eased the second Emma stepped into the kitchen. The warmth, the odors, the easy chatter and laughter among the people gathered around the scarred oak farmhouse table was the total opposite of what she'd lived with for much of the past year.

"We have company," Damien said, interrupting chatter

that was so noisy no one had heard them come in through the mudroom and walk to the kitchen door.

Heads raised and immediately all pairs of eyes focused on Emma and Belle. Belle began to wiggle and fuss, sputtering cries that were likely the prelude to full-fledged bawling.

The two men pushed back from the table and stood in true Texas cowboy gentleman fashion. An attractive middle-age woman at the head of the table looked up. Her piercing gaze met with Emma's, and Emma's whisper of reprieve took a nosedive.

This was not a woman who'd be a pushover for Emma's lies. Nor would she welcome trouble into the midst of her family.

"This is Emma Smith," Damien said. "She drove up from Victoria to visit her aunt. Somehow she took a wrong turn and ended up on the logging road that runs parallel to Beaver Creek."

"What were you driving, a tank?" one of the men questioned. "The holes in that road would swallow a normal vehicle."

"Apparently one of them did," Damien explained. "The car is now likely sinking like quicksand."

Emma breathed easier. The explanation sounded far more feasible coming from Damien. She'd always been a rotten liar.

"Thankfully, I wandered into your pasture hoping to find help, and Damien came along," Emma said.

The woman who'd eyed her warily at first smiled as she stood and walked toward Emma. "We wondered where Damien had gotten off to. But when Tague checked and found his horse missing from the barn, we figured he'd gone out for one last check on the cattle."

"Lucky for me and Belle that he did."

"I'm Carolina Lambert, Damien's mother."

So he wasn't a simple cowboy. He was a Lambert. Obviously wealthy and likely powerful, yet he'd easily passed for your everyday wrangler. Already she loved Texas.

Carolina stood, walked over and leaned in for a closer look at the squirming infant, whose face was turning redder by the second.

"Oh, poor little sweetheart. You must be cold. We'll take care of that." Carolina looked up. "She's adorable."

"Thank you."

Damien made quick introductions of the rest of the people at the table as Belle tuned up. The two men were his brothers, Durk and Tague. Both were tanned and muscular and shared Damien's good looks. Tague sported a ready smile. Durk eyed her suspiciously, his handshake firm.

Damien's grandma Pearl was silver-haired, petite and wrinkled but with a mischievous sparkle in her violet eyes. His aunt Sybil looked to be in her sixties. She wore heavy makeup and her neck and wrists were weighted down with chunky silver and turquoise jewelry. A black wig topped her head like a hat. Emma hoped hers was not nearly so conspicuous.

"You're the best-looking stray Damien's ever come home with," Tague said. "Of course, your closest competition was a mangy yellow dog with a bad drool."

"Glad I beat that out." She managed a smile.

"Have a seat," Grandma Pearl said. "You need some soup to warm you up. A little sherry wouldn't hurt, either."

"Mother thinks sherry is the cure for everything," Sybil said. "I'll get you some soup."

"Maybe we should give Emma a chance to catch her breath and warm up before we start pushing food on her," Carolina said.

Belle began to wail.

"Why don't you let me take her for you," Carolina said. "You must be exhausted."

"She's hungry," Emma said. "I really need to feed her."

"Of course. And I'm sure you'd appreciate some privacy," Carolina said. "Come with me to the family room. There's a rocker near the fireplace."

Emma took a deep breath, preparing herself for the next lie. Nothing about this was going to be easy, but it was still a million times better than freezing to death or being violated by Julio.

"I know how irresponsible this sounds, but I was so upset when I walked away from the truck that I left Belle's bottles of formula behind."

Durk's eyebrows arched. "I thought you said you were driving a car."

"It's an SUV," she said, as if that explained it. "Anyway, it's imperative that I go into town and get bottles and formula for her."

"No use to go into town for that," Carolina said. "My neighbor Karen has a son about the same size as your Belle. She's over frequently since we're both on the library committee and planning a new extension. I keep bottles and formula here for her. Disposable diapers, as well."

"She uses Similac," Sybil said. "What kind of formula do you use with Belle?"

"Similac."

"Now, that's luck," Sybil said.

Grandma Pearl clicked her tongue against her false teeth. "Luck has nothing to do with it. The Lord works in mysterious ways."

"Indeed he does," Carolina agreed.

"I'll go stoke the fire," Tague said.

Carolina walked over to the counter. "I'll get a bottle ready."

"I don't want to interrupt your dinner," Emma said. "Just point me to the formula and I'll take care of feeding Belle."

"Nonsense," Carolina said. "I've finished my soup. And dessert and coffee can wait until you're ready to join us. I'll get the bottle. You just take Belle to the fire so the both of you can get warm."

"Thanks so much," Emma said. "And thankfully we're warmer already. My teeth have totally stopped chattering."

"Did you say you have false teeth?" Pearl asked.

"No," Emma said. "My real ones were chattering from the cold."

"Mother, are you wearing your hearing aids?" Sybil asked.

Pearl smiled. "I might have left them on my dressing table."

"Do I just follow the directions on the can of formula?" Carolina asked.

"Yes. And you can't imagine how I appreciate this."

Unexpected tears began to well at the back of her eyes. Simple acts of kindness and words of faith had become foreign to her. Now they were warming her heart and making her feel guilty at the same time.

Grandma Pearl left the table and joined them at the counter. "Don't you think you should call your aunt?"

"I will once I've fed Belle. She's not actually expecting me until tomorrow, but when the weather forecast said snow in Dallas tonight, I decided to come up a day early. I'd planned to make it before dark, but the Friday afternoon traffic was much worse than I'd expected."

"Is that blood on your arm?" Sybil asked.

Emma had tried to position the rebozo so that no one would notice the blood, but there was no hiding the fact now.

"I scratched my arm while climbing through the fence," she said. "I'm sure it's nothing to be concerned about."

"It looks like you lost a lot of blood to me," Sybil said. "You better let someone take a look at it."

"It's okay, really."

"It needs to be checked," Damien said, the authority in his voice leaving little room for argument.

"Okay," she agreed. "As soon as I finish feeding Belle."

"Perhaps you shouldn't wait that long," Carolina said. "You may still be losing blood. Sybil and I can handle feeding Belle or at least get started at it while Damien checks your injury. There's a fully stocked first-aid kit in the hall bathroom."

"Tague, how about taking care of King for me?" Damien asked. "I left her just outside the back door."

"No problem. I'll tuck her in for the night."

Reluctantly, Emma unwound Belle from the folds of cloth so that she could hand the baby to Carolina. Placing Belle in Carolina's hands made her uneasy, though Carolina surely knew more about tending to a baby's needs than Emma did.

What she knew about babies could be composed in a tweet.

A tweet. It had been months since she'd even thought about that social form of communication. Caudillo had made sure she hadn't had access to the internet, a phone or anything else that could have connected her to the outside world.

He, on the other hand, came and went freely on his yacht and small plane as if he were your ordinary multibillionaire CEO.

When Emma looked up, her nerves tightened to coiled

steel. The look in Damien's eyes said he had more on his mind than first aid.

He hadn't given her away, but he was not fooled by her performance. She'd be lucky if he didn't call the sheriff and have her picked up before he bandaged her arm.

Chapter Three

Emma followed Damien down the hallway to the sounds of Carolina crooning to Belle behind them.

She glanced around the room. Heavy wooden bookshelves lined two walls, and bulbs of blooming paper-white narcissus rested on a wide window ledge. The drapes were open, revealing a glimpse of falling snow.

Emma suspected it was Carolina's taste that spilled so gracefully over the decor—soft, earthy colors, intricate moldings, paintings of hunting dogs on the walls. Silver-framed family pictures were scattered like valuable trinkets among the books.

Damien motioned her to an overstuffed armchair in a muted plaid that sat near the window next to a beautifully crafted antique end table. She rearranged the throw pillows and settled into the chair, certain her web of lies was going to spin out of control at any minute.

"There's no use for you to bother with this," she said. "If you'll point me to the bathroom and give me a Band-Aid and a tube of antiseptic, I can take care of it myself."

"Remove the shawl."

Damien's tone suggested he was used to being in control, or perhaps he was just tired of playing rescuer. She yanked impatiently at the wrap, tightening instead of loosening the knot that had secured Belle.

"Let me help you with that," Damien said, his tone not quite as brusque as before. Before she could protest, he leaned in close and his hands brushed hers as he took hold of the looped fabric.

His touch ripped along her nerves, partly the automatic cringe she'd developed to the nearness of Caudillo. But there was also a heady factor involved that she couldn't explain, perhaps an instinctive reaction of a desperate woman to her rescuer.

"You're as tangled as a calf in a downed mesquite tree," Damien quipped.

"I'm sorry. Just cut it. It's going straight to the trash anyway."

"Good idea." He walked to a mahogany desk on the other side of the room and took a pair of scissors from the top drawer. "You might have bled a lot more if you hadn't had the shawl putting pressure against the cut."

"I'm surprised it bled as much as it did," she said. "I'm sure the cut isn't bad or I'd be in a lot more pain."

"If that's the case, I'll just clean the injury, apply some antiseptic, bandage the tear and you'll be back in business. But I'm guessing it's going to need stitches."

Stitches were not an option. She couldn't deal with all the questions the E.R. personnel would ask. Besides, she no longer had health insurance, and even if she had, she couldn't give them her real name.

The money she'd stolen from Caudillo wouldn't last long if she started paying for visits to the E.R.

"Stitches at this time of night would require a trip to an emergency room," she argued. "You said yourself it's not safe to drive the roads."

"I'm not planning to drive to an E.R. Doc Benson lives on an adjoining spread. We can get there by a four-wheeler if we have to."

"I'm sure the doctor doesn't work from his living room."

"He usually works from my barn, but he'll likely make an exception in your case."

"From your barn?"

"Yep. He's an equine vet, best one in the county. Sewing a few stitches in you would be easy work. I'm guessing you don't have the kick of a pissed-off quarter horse."

The vet would no doubt provide better medical care than she'd have gotten with Caudillo. She'd contracted some type of viral infection in September that had sent her fever soaring so high she'd become delusional. Even then he hadn't taken her to a doctor.

Fortunately, the sickness ran its course and she recovered with no lasting effects except a stronger determination than ever to escape the monster.

Damien cut through the fabric and the shawl finally fell loose—all except the last layers of cotton that were soaked with blood. Finally, even that was removed and she got her first look at the injury.

The wound gaped open, revealing exposed tissue. She swallowed hard, fighting off a wave of nausea.

"You definitely need stitches," Damien said. "But I've never seen a tear from barbed wire that was this clean-cut. It looks more like it was done with a surgeon's scalpel or at least a very sharp knife." Suspicion edged his voice.

"My one small glimmer of luck," Emma said. "A clean cut will make it easier to stitch and heal."

She tried to sound confident, although she was shaking inside. Julio could have easily killed her and Belle in that truck or in the woods if he'd caught up with her. Now that she was thinking more clearly, she found it almost impossible to believe she'd escaped him or Caudillo.

She was a living miracle, and she planned to do whatever it took to keep on living. If that meant lying to Damien, so be it. If it meant spitting in the face of the devil himself, she'd do that, too.

Damien leaned in closer. "How did you really wind up in my pasture tonight?"

"I explained all of that. I was searching for help."

"Look at me, Emma."

She forced herself to meet his steely gaze.

"Tell me the truth. Did someone do this to you?"

"No one attacked me," she said.

"You don't have to be afraid to tell the truth."

Maybe not in Damien's world. "I've told you the truth."

"Okay," he acknowledged, although it was clear he wasn't buying it. "I'll give Doc Benson a call. It may be a while before he can see you, so we should go ahead and clean and bandage the wound. Have you had a tetanus booster lately?"

"Last March."

"Was that because of an injury?"

"No. I was traveling out of the country...." Another slip. There was nothing to do but finish the statement. "I was just going on vacation, but my doctor checked my records and recommended the booster."

"Where did you go?"

"Italy," she lied. Too bad she hadn't gone there like she'd originally planned instead of letting her friend Dorothy talk her into island-hopping in the Caribbean.

"Okay, let's go to the bathroom and get this cleaned up."

Once in the bathroom, Damien excused himself for a minute to make a quick call to his vet friend. She stared out the window, thinking how changed the world looked when coated with snow. That's what she needed—a way to white out the ugliness she'd endured these past months, a chance to go on with her life.

Damien returned quickly and slipped his hands into a pair of latex gloves.

"Good news. You don't have to get out in the cold again. Benson's coming here. In the meantime, he said to flush the wound with a saline solution and wash it with Betadine."

"Do you have that on hand?"

"Yep. And he said to be careful with the arm and eat some of Mother's soup. You need the nourishment.

"Oh, and Mother said to tell you that she'd bring you a sweat suit if you want to wash up and change into something dry and comfortable before you eat. The clothes are hers, so they'll be a little large."

"That would be great."

She sat perfectly still as he washed the blood and the grime of the day from the area around the cut. She contemplated the strange turn of events. An hour ago, she'd been freezing cold and cloaked in fear and dread. Now she was being catered to and tended as if she were a princess who'd been dropped into a cowboy castle—even if the prince didn't totally believe her.

A few days of this and her belief in the goodness of man might make a comeback. But she didn't have a few days. She'd have to leave first thing in the morning, before Damien discovered that there was no car in a ditch anywhere near where he'd found her.

In the meantime, she might as well enjoy her freedom and the comfort the Lamberts provided. Even if all she had to offer in return was lies.

DAMIEN HAD KNOWN BLAKE Benson since they were in fifth grade and Blake's father had bought the small spread that backed up to theirs. They'd been best friends all through school, even shared a condo the first two years they were at Texas A&M University.

They'd hunted together, fished together, drunk together and had a few major disagreements—mostly over politics or love. In college, they had tended to fall for the same females.

That was no longer a concern, since Blake was happily married and the father of three. Damien had practically given up hope of finding a woman he wanted to roll in the hay with until they were too old for rolling or pitching hay.

Other than his brothers, there wasn't a man on earth Damien trusted more than Blake. Now that Emma was stitched and back in the kitchen with Carolina, Damien was eager to hear what Blake had to say about her and her injury. But first, the necessary small talk.

"How's the family?" Damien asked as he walked Blake to his black pickup truck.

"Sylvia's great. She's deliriously excited about the prospect of helping the twins build their first snowman."

"And the baby?"

"Jenna's a handful. She's teething, and little miss prima donna is making sure we all know that she doesn't like discomfort."

"Isn't she a little young to get teeth?"

"She's six months. Scooting around at the speed of light and with an attitude."

"And has her dad wrapped around her finger."

"You know it. So tell me about Emma Smith."

"You know as much as I do," Damien admitted.

"A sexy phantom who appeared in your pasture on a snowy night? That's the stuff of fantasies."

"If you leave out the part about having a baby and the suspicious tale of a ditched car and tearing her arm on the barbed wire."

"I have to admit that I've never seen that exact kind of injury from getting caught on a barb."

"I thought the same thing," Damien said. "I questioned her about it, but she didn't budge."

"What do you think happened?" Blake asked.

"My guess is that she had a fight with a violent husband or boyfriend who kicked her out of the car."

"That would have to be a mean son of a bitch to toss a woman and a baby out on a night like this," Blake said.

"Or someone so high on booze or drugs that he didn't realize the seriousness of his actions."

"Emma seems too classy to hang out with trash like that," Blake said. "Good manners, better grammar than me, a lady all the way. Mysterious and damn good-looking."

"You noticed."

"I'm married, not dead."

"I'm not dead, either, but I'm not buying her story." He was intrigued by Emma, though, and not sure why. In his book, lying was one of the biggest turnoffs around—unless she had a very good reason. Like fear of the man who had sliced his brand into her arm.

"One thing for sure, Carolina is taken with that baby," Blake said. "She even called Sylvia and asked her to send over some of Jenna's outgrown baby clothes. Sylvia had me bring a boxful with me."

"You know Mother. She can't resist a good charity case—or a baby."

Blake opened the truck door and tossed his black satchel to the passenger seat. "I don't look for Emma to have any trouble with the arm, but she should probably get it checked out tomorrow just in case. She might even appreciate a people doc."

"I'll take her into urgent care out on the highway once the roads clear up."

"And keep me posted on the continuing saga of Cowboy Rescues Mysterious Woman and Child."

"You mean, like whether or not there really is a car in a ditch on a road Emma should have never been on?"

"That, and what it's like sleeping with a beautiful stranger."

"You *are* into fantasies tonight."

"Snow makes me a romantic, which is why I'm heading straight home to my own gorgeous wife."

Damien stood in the falling snow as Blake drove away, his mind cluttered with the strange turn the evening had taken. The birth certificate that created troubling doubts. A rescue in the snow.

The first could hopefully be cleared up with a conversation when things settled down and he had some time alone with his mother. As for the mystery surrounding Emma Smith, that wasn't really his concern.

He'd brought her and her baby to the house. They were warm and safe. That should be the end of his involvement.

So why couldn't he shake her and her problems from his mind?

CAROLINA OPENED THE DOOR and ushered Emma into the first-floor guest suite. It was in the west wing of the sprawling house, away from the living area and the noise that entailed, and with a terrific view of the swimming pool and its surrounding gardens.

The suite had been two small rooms when she'd married Hugh, and the pool had been an ugly concrete hole in the ground with no redeeming features. Still, the house and everything about the Bent Pine Ranch had seemed incredibly luxurious to Carolina.

Emma paused in the doorway, a sleeping Belle cradled

in her arms. "This is where you want me to spend the night?"

"Is something wrong, dear?"

"No. I'm awed. This is like something from a home-decorating magazine—only far more inviting."

"I like to make my guests comfortable," Carolina said, pleased that Emma appreciated the efforts she'd put into creating the hideaway.

"I'm afraid I'm more an intruder than a guest," Emma said.

"Nonsense. You were unexpected, but you and Belle brightened a cold, snowy night. I shudder to think what might have happened if Damien hadn't gone out one last time and run into you. It was meant to be."

Carolina crossed the room and touched the back of the antique cradle that had been handed down through three generations of Lamberts. "I hope Belle likes her accommodations."

Emma stared at the cradle, obviously noticing it for the first time. She sucked her bottom lip into her mouth, and Carolina could see the moisture glistening in her soft violet eyes.

"I've never seen anything like that. It's fit for a princess."

"My husband's grandfather made it for his children, and every Lambert offspring since has slept in it. It's had to be repaired and refinished a time or two over the years, but it's held up amazingly well. I thought it would be perfect for Belle."

"You surely didn't get it out of storage just for one night?"

"No. I have a room upstairs where I keep some of the family heirlooms on display. Hugh's grandfather was a master craftsman, and some of the toys he made his children are not only inventive but amazing. There's a giant rocking horse that almost looks like a real pony. Damien spent hours on it long before he was able to ride a real horse on his own."

"I'd love to see it."

"I'll give you the full tour tomorrow morning. Now you probably need some rest. Your private bath is through this door," Carolina said, opening the door to reveal the curtained claw-foot tub and the dressing table.

"The cabinet is stocked with staples, but if you need anything else, just let me know. And I hung your freshly laundered clothes in the closet and put Belle's dress in the chest along with the extra outfits Sylvia sent over and a supply of diapers."

"You think of everything."

"I'm a stickler for details. It's the curse that causes me to sit on far too many committees. Oh, and feel free to use the phone. I know you'll want to connect with your aunt in the morning. There's a phone book in the bedside table if you need it."

"Thanks. In case I do get in touch with my aunt and she wants to pick me up, how would I tell her to get to the ranch?"

"She can ask anyone in the area where Bent Pine Ranch is. They'll be able to give her directions. Or..." Carolina opened the top drawer of an antique chest and took out a box of stationery engraved with the Bent Pine brand and a small-scale map showing directions to the ranch from I-35 and I-45. The ranch fell about halfway between the two interstate highways. "The address is on this stationery, along with easy-to-follow directions."

Emma lay Belle in the cradle atop the clean, specially made sheet. Belle barely stirred. She looked like an angel in the pink footed onesie that Sylvia had sent over.

Carolina touched the tiny hand and memories flooded her mind. The night she'd placed Damien in this same crib for the very first time—the night she and Hugh had married. She'd had tears that night. Her heart had been so full.

Hugh had laughed at her, but he'd quickly become as attached to their miracle son as she was.

Hugh. The only man she'd ever loved. She missed him so, but she treasured every second they'd had together. He'd been a hardheaded man, never comfortable showing his emotions—except with her. She'd been his one weak spot. He'd been her strength.

"I should go and let you get some sleep," Carolina said.

"I am tired," Emma admitted. "And that bed looks so tempting I can't wait to crawl between the sheets. I know I've said it a half-dozen times tonight, but I can't tell you how much I appreciate your hospitality."

Carolina's hand closed around the doorknob, but she hesitated. "You know, Emma, I have this feeling that God sent you to us tonight—as much for us as for you. Sleep tight."

EMMA DROPPED TO THE BED as the door closed behind Carolina. She'd never met a family like the Lamberts. That would make it doubly hard to leave in the morning. But with luck she'd be out of here before Damien decided to go look for her ditched car. The plan was already worked out in her mind.

There was just one last detail to take care of. She picked up the phone and made a call that would put her plan in motion.

Once she'd showered, she snuggled under the covers and closed her eyes. She expected to see Caudillo's image waiting for her in the dark with angry threats of what he'd do to her for escaping his paradise prison.

But it was Damien's face that appeared as she drifted into a sound, safe sleep.

Chapter Four

Caudillo paced the tiled floor of his office. "I leave for a few days, and you let marauders take everything, even my beloved Emma."

"What could we do? They came onto the island with hundreds of armed men."

"You could have fought to the death instead of hiding."

"We fought, but there were so many of them."

"You are the leader of a hundred men, Chale, armed with the best weapons money can buy. You should have been able to shoot them like ducks in a row as they stepped off their ship. You let down your guard while I was away. Admit it, Chale."

"I can only speak for myself. I was not on guard duty that night."

"But you are responsible for your men, and you were responsible for keeping my island safe."

Chale straightened the bandoleer that crossed over his shoulder, as if his supply of cartridges mattered now.

"I assumed my orders were being obeyed."

"You assumed? I could train a monkey to assume and do nothing. And now not only are crates of weapons missing, but Emma is gone, as well."

"I will see that she is found, unless she is in the stomach of a shark."

"No, Chale. You will not. You have lost my trust. You are relieved of duty."

Sweat pooled on Chale's forehead and circled the armpits of his white shirt. Another time, Caudillo would have enjoyed his sniveling fear. Today, there was too much at stake to enjoy anything.

"Emma was not just another concubine, Chale. She is brilliant and deductive. She knows too much. Her freedom could bring the end of mine."

Not that Caudillo would let it go that far. But that didn't excuse Chale's negligence.

Chale fell to his knees. "Please, Caudillo. Let me make this up to you. Let me find her. I know I can."

"Good night, Chale. I'm sorry our arrangement must end this way."

"May I leave the island?"

"Of course. You are free to go."

"Thank you, sir." Chale stood and walked toward the door. Caudillo waited until his hand was on the doorknob. Then he lifted his pistol and fired one shot into the back of Chale's head.

That done, he picked up his phone and made a call.

"I told you to never call me at this number."

"We have a problem."

"What kind of problem?"

"Emma Muran has escaped the island."

"How did you let that happen?"

"I trusted the wrong person. That's been taken care of."

"Do you have reason to believe she's in the United States?"

"If not, she will be soon. She's a brilliant woman. She'd find a way to get home."

"I'll do what I can, but the best option is for you to find

her and take her back to the island before she goes to the
American authorities."

"I don't want her back. I want her dead. If I go down,
so will you."

Caudillo broke the connection and beat a fist into the
wall. Emma could have had it all. He'd gone after her for
purely selfish reasons, but his heart had found in her everything it desired.

She'd crushed it. Now she could crush him. He would
not let that happen. He was Caudillo.

EMMA JERKED AWAKE TO AN anxiety attack that sent her
pulse skyrocketing and her stomach churning. It took several agonizing seconds for her to realize where she was.

Belle began to fuss, soft grunting sounds that had probably been the impetus that stirred Emma from sleep. She
rolled over, kicked off the covers and threw her feet over
the side of the cloud-soft mattress.

"Are you hungry again?" she crooned to Belle. Or
maybe she was sick. What if the formula had given her
colic? And if it had, what was Emma supposed to do about
that?

Most women had at least nine months to get up to speed
on their mothering skills. Emma had been granted seconds. One moment Belle's mother had been alive, the next
she was dead. But at least Belle had one real parent out
there. The sooner Emma found Juan Perez, the better.

She peered down at Belle. The squirming infant was
working at getting both balled fists into her mouth.

"I'm going to take that for hunger," Emma crooned.
"And we have formula for you right down the hallway."

Emma pulled on the buttery-soft sweats Carolina had
lent her and then leaned over to pick up Belle. As she did,
she remembered the horrid wig.

It was still dark out, but that didn't guarantee that someone else might not get out of bed and wander into the kitchen. No chance they wouldn't notice that her hair had changed from long and black to chin length and blond.

She plopped the wig onto her head, tucked loose blond hairs beneath it and then picked up Belle and started to the kitchen. The soft glow of night-lights scattered about the hallway lit her path.

Emma tiptoed, hoping not to wake anyone else in the house, but the occasional groan of a floorboard seemed almost deafening in the silence. She was relieved to make it to the kitchen without Belle starting to wail.

"Feeding time?"

Emma spun around at the voice, stubbing the big toe on her right foot against a chair. She sucked in her breath at the quick flash of pain and did a fast and unbalanced two-step.

"Sorry. I didn't mean to startle you," Damien said, his whispered voice still raspy from sleep.

"I wasn't expecting anyone else to be up," she said. "And I didn't see you in the dark."

"I woke up and couldn't get back to sleep. I got up for a glass of milk and ended up standing here watching it snow."

"It's beautiful," she said. "Like frosting for the earth."

Damien clicked on the low lights beneath the top cabinets. "Can I help you with something?"

"You can hold Belle while I mix her formula."

"Are you sure you trust me with her? The babies I'm used to dealing with have four legs and weigh a lot more."

Having taken care of any kind of baby put him one up on Emma. "Sit down first," she said, "and I'll hand her to you." She fit the baby into his arms. An unfamiliar sensation zinged through her senses. She did her best to ignore it, but it lingered even when she'd walked away from Damien.

Once the bottle was ready, Emma took Belle from Damien and carried her to the rocker in the family room. The ashes in the fireplace still gave off a glow and a shimmer of heat. But even without that, the room was comfortable. And the light drifting from the kitchen gave off just enough illumination.

Damien joined her in the family room a minute later. She upped her guard, determined not to let his virility and protectiveness ignite any repeat sensations or increase in pulse.

Damien leaned against the hearth and looked down at her and Belle. "Did you call your husband and let him know you were safe?"

"I'm a single mom." She assumed he and his family had figured that out from the absence of a wedding ring and the fact that she hadn't mentioned a spouse. Damien was likely just fishing for information now, though she wasn't sure why he'd care.

"What about Belle's father?" he asked.

"We never married. Let's just say I have bad luck in choosing men." That part was definitely true. "What about you?" she asked. "Have you ever been married?"

"No. Guess you could say women have good luck in avoiding me."

She doubted that. Rich. Rugged good looks. Hard bodied. Intelligent. That was not the kind of man women avoided.

"What about your father?" she asked. "No one's mentioned him, but your mother wears a wedding band."

"Dad died three months ago. He was flying home from a Cowboys game with some friends, and their small plane went down in a storm."

"I'm so sorry for all of you. Poor Carolina. She must feel lost without him."

"She does, but she has incredible strength."

"I can tell, and an amazing spirit. I felt it the first time I saw her."

"Mother was delighted to have you and Belle here tonight."

"She took excellent care of us."

"Give her a cause or someone to help and she throws herself into the task."

"I have to admit that I've never met a family like yours, Damien. I'm a complete stranger, and yet you've all treated me like part of the family."

"Rescuing a woman in distress is the cowboy way. So why don't you tell me what really happened to your arm, Emma."

Back to that. She should have known this was more than a casual conversation. "I *have* told you."

"Who attacked you?"

She felt a traitorous urge to give him what he wanted, to just open her mouth and let the whole sordid tale spill out. But she didn't dare. For his and his family's safety as much as her own.

"Does it really matter, Damien? I'm leaving in the morning and you'll never see me or have to worry about me again."

"You don't have to go."

"Are you suggesting I stay? Why?"

"I think you're in some kind of trouble and need help."

She had to admit that it would be heaven to have a man like him to protect her.

Only he couldn't. Even Damien Lambert was no match for Caudillo.

"I appreciate the concern, but you've read things all

wrong. I truly appreciate your help tonight, but there's no point in my staying."

"If you change your mind, the offer still stands." With that, he walked away.

EMMA WOKE AS THE FIRST rays of sun peeked over the horizon and sent brilliant spikes of light across the bed. She turned quickly to check the time, panicky that the alarm she'd set for seven-thirty had failed to go off.

Twenty-eight past seven. All was well. She punched the button to cancel the alarm and then rolled out of bed quickly to check on Belle. The infant was sleeping peacefully.

Perfect. That would give Emma time to get dressed before she had to give Belle her bottle. The car and driver she'd hired would be here at nine to pick up her and Belle and drive them into Dallas, unless the icy conditions closed the roads. In that case, the driver would be here as soon as he could make it.

Emma hesitated just long enough to glance out the window. The garden area had been transformed to a winter wonderland. Her awe at the beauty shifted to apprehension. What if the driver couldn't get here for hours? What if Damien insisted on taking one of his four-wheelers to check on her car?

She couldn't stay here once her lies were exposed. It was difficult enough merely facing Damien's suspicions.

Belle was rooting around in the cradle by the time Emma was dressed. Emma watched her, her heart aching for the mother Belle had lost. For a second she wondered what would happen if she couldn't find Belle's father. She definitely couldn't desert the child.

Except that Emma was running for her life, and if she

failed to locate Juan Perez, she'd have no choice but to depend on social services to find Belle a loving home.

Only that didn't always happen. Emma knew that all too well.

Emma picked up Belle and cuddled her against her chest as she kissed the top of the Belle's sweet head. "I won't abandon you, sweetheart. I'll find your daddy. I don't know how, but I will. I won't give up until I do."

Belle stretched and started poking her fists into her mouth again.

"Okay, so you're worried about the more pressing needs of the moment—like food. I can handle that, too. Thanks to the Lamberts."

Enticing odors of coffee and bacon met Emma's nostrils before she neared the kitchen. But it was the voices that captured her attention. She found herself listening for Damien's. She didn't hear him, but that didn't mean he wasn't there.

She concentrated on what she had to say and forced a smile to her lips as she stepped into the kitchen.

"There you two are," Carolina greeted, "just in time for breakfast."

Emma scanned the room. Grandma Pearl and Sybil were both seated on one side of the long table, which was laden with eggs over-easy, steaming grits, crisp bacon, link sausage and a huge stack of pancakes.

Carolina scooted between Pearl and Sybil and added a warmer of syrup and a plate of butter to the mix.

"I seem to have an uncanny talent for appearing just in time to eat," Emma said.

"That doesn't take a lot of talent around here," Tague said. "We spend a lot of time at the table. How about coffee?"

"Coffee sounds great."

Belle began to fuss.

"We haven't forgotten about you," Emma said. "Your breakfast is coming up."

"I'll mix her formula while you drink your coffee," Carolina said.

"You've probably done most of the cooking," Emma protested. "You should eat while the food is hot."

"I cooked the eggs," Grandma Pearl said. "Hugh always said I was the best egg cook west of the Mississippi."

"And Dad was right," Tague said as he handed Emma her coffee.

"There's sugar and cream on the counter," Sybil said.

"Thanks, but I take it plain and black."

Both Damien and Durk were conspicuously missing from the family meal. Emma resisted asking about Damien, but she couldn't keep from eyeing the door.

"Damien and Durk took four-wheelers out to check on the livestock," Carolina offered.

"They just wanted to play in the snow," Sybil said. "They better get back in here if they don't want to miss breakfast."

Damien and Durk entered a few minutes later as if on cue, their faces red from the wind and cold. Damien met her gaze and a fluttering sensation swept through her. If it was attraction, it couldn't have picked a worse time to surface.

"Food," Durk said. "And I'm famished. Damien's had me out working since sunup."

"I don't want you to forget the joys of ranching."

"Riding those toys is not work," Pearl said. "Back when your grandpa was ranching, he relied on horses instead of those noisy contraptions."

Damien touched his grandmother on the shoulder as he made his way to the table. "Bet you'll change your mind about my new four-wheeler when I take you for a ride on it."

"Pshaw." Pearl patted her puff of silvery-gray hair. "You won't ever catch me on one of those senseless contrivances."

Carolina returned to the table with a filled baby bottle. She set the bottle down next to Emma and turned to Damien. "Would you say grace?"

All heads bowed and the room fell silent except for Belle's grunts and coos. Damien's strong hand reached down and wrapped around Emma's free one. A blush burned in her cheeks until she realized that everyone at the table had joined hands.

Damien's strong voice filled the room. Warmth suffused Emma, along with a sense of rightness with the world that she hadn't felt in years.

She knew she still had a long way to go before she'd feel safe or have any kind of peace. Caudillo had made certain of that. But hopefully this was the first step toward finding her way again.

"May I feed Belle?" Carolina asked, after Damien's amen. "I munched while I cooked, so I'm not really hungry."

"If you'd like to," Emma said. It was the least she could do. Besides, she'd be on her own with Belle once the car arrived, and by night she'd likely be wishing for help with her.

Emma waited until they were almost finished with the meal before making the announcement that she'd been reviewing in her mind.

"I called my aunt. She insisted that my uncle drive out and pick me up this morning. I'm expecting him about nine unless the roads are impassable."

"I'll hate to see you go," Carolina said, "but I know your aunt must be eager to see you."

"She is, but I assured her that you were the most gracious hosts a wounded traveler could hope for. Oh, and she said that my uncle will check on the car and have it towed, if necessary."

"Sounds as if you have everything under control," Damien said. He pushed back from the table. "If you'll excuse me, I still need to feed and water the horses."

Her heart sank at the careless goodbye.

But it was for the best. No more zings of attraction to send her on a shaky emotional high. No more illusions.

No more Damien.

The phone rang as he carried his empty plate to the sink.

Carolina looked up from feeding Belle. "Can you get that, Damien?"

"Sure thing." He picked up the cordless extension, glanced at the caller ID and then left the room before answering.

Emma glanced at her watch. It was twenty minutes before nine.

"THIS IS KELLY'S CHAUFFEUR Service. I'm supposed to pick up Emma Smith at Bent Pine Ranch this morning at nine o'clock, but there's a major pileup out here on Interstate 35. Nothing's moving. I mean nothing. It's been one fender bender after another all morning."

So there was no uncle driving out to pick Emma up. Another lie. But why? Was Emma afraid or just a psychopathic liar?

"I'll see that she gets the message," Damien said.

"I'm really supposed to talk directly to the passenger in a situation like this."

"She's not available right now. Why don't you call back closer to nine?"

"I suppose I can do that. Tell her I'll be there whenever I can, but I suspect it will be closer to ten than nine. It might even be later."

"I'm sure she'll understand." And Damien planned to understand a lot more himself before this was over. He started back to the kitchen. There would be a confrontation. Whether or not it was private would be up to Emma.

The doorbell rang. What now?

He strode back through the den and into the foyer. When he opened the door, Sheriff Garcia stared back at him, a grim turn to his ruddy mouth.

The sheriff worried the brim of his worn Stetson. "Morning, Damien."

"Good morning, Sheriff. You look like a man who could use a cup of hot coffee and one of Mother's pancakes."

"I could use them, but there's no time for that this morning."

"Guess the weather is playing havoc with the traffic."

"Nope. It's the idiots who don't know how to drive in this weather that cause the problems. But that's not why I'm here."

"So what's up?"

"The Dobson boys were out on their four-wheelers this morning." His tone was grim.

"Was there an accident?"

"No, but while they were out, they spotted a truck hooked up to a trailer. The tops were covered in snow like they had been there all night."

"Was anybody around?"

"No one was in the cab," the sheriff continued, "but the back door of the trailer was open. Naturally, they jumped in to look around, especially since no one uses that old logging road but them."

"The old logging road that borders my property?"

"That's the one. In fact, they found the truck near where the road skirts Beaver Creek."

Damien's attention piqued. "Are you sure they said truck and not an SUV?"

"It was a truck, all right—with a body inside the back lying in a pool of blood."

Damien's stomach clenched. This was too close to where he'd found Emma. There was no way it could not be related. "Have you been to the site?"

"Just left there. Man had a knife right through his chest."

"Murder?"

"Looks that way. There was blood leading away from the truck and into the woods. Whoever did him in must have gotten cut in the scuffle."

Damien's mind rocked with sickening possibilities. He'd been suspicious of the ditched-car story, but murder had never crossed his mind. "I don't suppose you spotted any other vehicles in the area."

"Not even a tire track. I don't think that road's been used in at least a year, unless it was by some druggies looking for a quiet place to get high."

And this might be drug related, as well. But Emma had not been on drugs last night when he'd found her.

"I hated to interrupt you knowing this weather would be keeping you busy," Garcia said, "but I thought I oughtta let you and your family know since it happened so close to your house. I figured you'd want to keep your eyes and ears open for trouble."

"I appreciate that," Damien said, though the warning had come a little late.

The sheriff looked past him and over his right shoulder. "I didn't realize you had company. Hope I didn't scare her with murder talk."

Damien turned and spotted Emma standing several feet away. He didn't know how much she'd heard, but from the ghostly pallor of her face, he'd say she'd heard enough.

"If you spot anyone in the area who looks suspicious, give me a call," the sheriff said.

"Count on it." But first Damien would get a few answers of his own.

He closed the door and turned toward Emma. She didn't move or blink an eye. It was as if she were in shock, but he didn't trust her appearance any more than he trusted her words. Not now.

"We need to talk, Emma. This time in my room, where we won't be disturbed. And no more lies. The party's over."

Chapter Five

Julio was dead and the weapon that had killed him was no doubt the same one that had inflicted the wound on her arm.

Emma's legs felt weak and rubbery, but somehow she managed to move them enough to be led by Damien. Even her breath seemed to be suspended until he pushed her into a room and closed the door behind them.

Finally anger broke through the shock. "I didn't kill Julio. I couldn't have. The knife was never in my hand."

"But that is your blood in the truck?"

"Yes. It's my blood, because the low-down, degenerate creep attacked me with his knife."

"Why did you lie about how you were injured?"

"Because I didn't want you or anyone else to know I'd ever been in that stinking truck. And don't take that condescending tone with me, Damien Lambert. You have no idea what I've been through."

She took a deep breath and fought off the budding hysteria and the hot tears burning in the corners of her eyes.

"If I sounded condescending, I'm sorry. But a man's been murdered, and to this point you've been feeding me nothing but lies."

"I didn't kill Julio, and that's the truth. I never intended to drag you into my problems. That's the truth, too. So pretend you never saw me. A car is picking me up any minute. Just let Belle and me get in it and ride away and I promise I'll never set foot on your ranch or in your life again."

He shook his head. "Not going to happen that way."

"It will be easier on both of us."

"I don't aid and abet murder suspects, Emma. And I don't believe in running from problems or hiding behind lies. Level with me and I might be able to help. Keep playing games, and I call Sheriff Garcia. Believe me, you'll like talking to me better than you will him."

"Trust me, Damien. You'd run, too, if you were in my shoes."

"You haven't given me one reason to trust you. And I'm not in your shoes. I'm in these boots that have tramped through more disgusting predicaments than you can count. I can handle whatever trouble you've got yourself into, as long as you're as innocent as you claim."

"Don't be so sure."

"Try me. What happened between you and this Julio guy who was murdered last night?"

She threw up her hands in frustration. She'd like nothing better than to spill her guts and get this all out in the open, but if she did she might as well stick a knife in her own chest. Still, Julio was dead and she was a suspect. She couldn't just walk away from that.

"Julio tried to rape me," she said, determined to keep this as simple as possible. "I tried to fight him off and got injured in the process. But I swear I never had my hands on that knife. I didn't kill him."

Unless… Her heart slammed against her chest as her mind circled a horrifying possibility.

Unless he'd fallen on his knife when she'd kicked his legs out from under him. That would explain why he hadn't come after her or shot her in the back.

"I didn't stab him," she repeated, but the conviction had gone out of her voice.

"Keep going."

"I kicked him and he went down. I took off running. I guess it's possible he fell on his knife, but my efforts were pure self-defense. There's no way I could have overpowered him. He's twice my size and I had Belle."

Damien's eyes bore into hers. "Did he rape you?" His voice had grown so husky, it didn't sound like him.

"No, but only because I got away." While he lay there bleeding to death. She felt sick to her stomach, and her nerves were so shaky she had to grab on to a bedpost for support.

Damien's fingers raked his thick, dark hair back from his forehead. "Is Julio Belle's father?"

"No. Thank God, no."

"So who was he?"

"He was the truck driver and the man in charge."

"In charge of what?"

This was where things were going to get sticky. She was innocent of murder, but crossing the border illegally was a crime even if she was an American citizen. The sheriff could arrest her and hold her for that.

He wouldn't, of course, if he knew the full story. But then the information about her kidnapping would go viral and Caudillo would make sure her freedom and her life came to an untimely end. But she had to give Damien an explanation that he'd buy.

"The truck carried illegal aliens across the border," she admitted.

"Human trafficking." Disgust colored Damien's voice. "Were there others on the truck when he tried to rape you?"

"No. He'd let them out, some just this side of the border,

some near the highway so that they could find their way to Dallas. He'd forced me to stay while he drove the truck to that deserted spot where I finally escaped."

"So what were you doing on the truck? You look and sound American to me."

"I am, and we should really just leave it at that."

"Nice try. Now, why were you on the truck?"

"I was…" She tried to come up with a reasonable explanation, but none came to mind.

"Did you work for the man who was murdered?"

"Absolutely not," she protested. "If you think I'm capable of being involved in an operation that treats people like cattle, then talking to you is a total waste of time."

"So why were you on the truck?"

"I swear I didn't kill Julio and I was a passenger on that truck for personal reasons. Can't we just let it go at that? If I tell you more, I'll just be dragging you into my problems."

"Damn it, Emma. I'm not worried about Julio. I'm worried about you and Belle, and if I was trying to avoid trouble, I'd have just turned you over to the sheriff. And you sure as hell don't have to protect me. I'm a big boy. I can handle myself."

He was big, muscular, strong and determined. And decent. That was the problem. Once she told him the truth, he wouldn't walk away.

He'd think he could save her from Caudillo, but he'd only put her, himself and possibly his wonderful family in jeopardy. "I can't draw you into this, Damien."

He pulled his cell phone from his pocket. "Then you leave me no choice but to call Sheriff Garcia so that he can arrest you."

The look in his eyes convinced her he wasn't bluffing. And if the sheriff put her under official arrest, how long would it take for Caudillo to realize that the Emma Smith accused of killing a human trafficker was really Emma Muran?

She dropped to the edge of the bed. "I should warn you that this is a very ugly, complex and convoluted story. And you have to promise me one thing."

"What's that?"

"That you won't get me killed so that you can be a hero."

"Being a hero is the furthest thing from my mind. And I've never thrown a woman to the wolves. I don't plan to start now."

She stared into space as the events of the past ten months replayed in her mind.

"You can start anytime," Damien said.

"I'm just trying to decide where to begin."

"You could start with taking off that ridiculous wig."

She ran her fingers through the wiry hair that touched her shoulder before trailing down her back. "You knew?"

"I did when you came into the kitchen last night with it hanging lopsided from your head."

Yet still he'd stayed up and offered to help her. Hopefully, he'd still feel that way after he knew the truth. She jerked the cheap, tacky wig from her head and tossed it onto the bed.

"You're a blonde?" he said.

"Yeah. Forget everything you've ever heard about them having more fun."

DAMIEN WAS TEMPTED TO GO over and sit beside Emma, but right now she was getting to him on so many levels he didn't trust himself to keep a clear head if he was that near her.

Emma pushed a lock of chin-length bobbed hair behind

her right ear. "It started as a planned two-week island-hopping adventure to the Caribbean with my friend and coworker Dorothy Paul."

"When was this?" Damien asked, trying to keep events clear in his mind.

"Last March. We'd been planning the trip for months, but two weeks before we were scheduled to go, Dorothy's car started giving her trouble. She decided to put the money she'd saved for vacation on a new car."

"So you went alone?"

"I did. That was mistake number one."

"I take it there were complications," he said, trying to get her to keep talking.

"Major complications, but not until five days into the trip. Up until then, I was having the time of my life, sipping tropical drinks in paradise and soaking up the sun on gorgeous strips of surf-washed sand."

And no doubt driving men wild with her blond hair and her great body in a tiny bikini. Better he didn't let his mind go there. "What happened to spoil the trip?"

"A private boat we'd charted ahead of time picked me up and took me to Misterioso Island, one of the few gems still mostly unspoiled by tourists."

"Where exactly is Misterioso?"

"It's part of the southern island chain in the Lesser Antilles, not far from Aruba and less than thirty miles from Venezuela. I fell in love with the island the second I stepped off the vessel. The hotel was a like a movie set, with wide verandas and flowers everywhere. And the sea was a shade of blue that was positively mystical."

"Sounds like heaven."

"Yes, but unfortunately, Misterioso turned out to be the entrance to hell."

Her shoulders slumped and a haunted look glazed her

eyes. Unless she was Oscar quality at faking emotions, she was telling the truth now, and reliving the events was taking its toll.

"If you'd like, I can get you some coffee, tea, water—or something a lot stronger."

"No. Just let me get through this before I crater and dissolve into tears or fury. I've had my share of both."

"Feel free to let it all hang out. This house has seen plenty of both over the years."

"Not like this. The first night on the island, I spotted this fabulous yacht anchored offshore. When I asked about it, the hotel staff eagerly filled me in on the details. The yacht's owner was a handsome and extremely wealthy entrepreneur who made infrequent stops at their island. But when he did, he created a stir."

"Big spender?"

"Always. He paid for everything in cash and left huge tips, sometimes as much as a hundred dollars for a drink, or what amounted to a hundred dollars had it been in American currency. That was a fortune to the lucky staff who received the generous tips. They fought to see who could do the most for him."

"Was he American?"

"No. European, a cosmopolitan mix of nationalities, I think."

"Did he speak English?"

"Fluently. And also Spanish, Portuguese, French, German, Italian and perhaps others. That's basically all I know of his background since he never shared personal information about himself. He thrived on combining the ostentatious with the clandestine. And on maintaining complete control of every aspect of his environment, including people."

"You still haven't mentioned his name."

"Because I hate even saying it out loud. And because telling you opens the door even wider for you to get involved in my problems and with this monster."

"I'm not going to do anything foolish." That was the best he could promise.

"Caudillo."

She spat it out as if it would burn if it lingered on her lips.

"A warlord," he said, acknowledging the word's meaning.

"Right, and it was an apt moniker for him, though I can think of a few others that would fit even better."

"Was that a first name or a last name?"

"It was the only name he ever used whenever I was around. I seriously doubt it was legitimate."

"So how did you hook up with him?"

"He had dinner on the island that first night. He invited me to his table, said it was bad luck to eat alone in paradise. Corny, I know, but I was in a fantasy-vacation frame of mind. At any rate, for the rest of the evening, he centered all his attention on me."

Damien pictured the two of them in the island paradise and couldn't help but feel a twinge of envy.

"We spent the next two days together," Emma continued, "walking on the beach, swimming in the surf, dining on seafood delicacies and sipping expensive wines that he supplied from his onboard selections. It was the perfect island experience. A bit surreal. Temporary. And seemingly harmless."

"I take it Caudillo had a darker side."

"Try midnight-black. But he was charming when it suited his purposes. It never once dawned on me that he already knew a lot about me or that my job back in Nashville was what attracted him to me."

This was growing more bizarre by the minute. "What's your job?"

"I *was* a tech agent with the Bureau of Alcohol, Tobacco, Firearms and Explosives."

"What specifically does a tech agent do?"

"They can have any number of duties. Mine was to track sales of automatic weapons and to report any suspicious or bulk movement of arms. I worked out of the Nashville office and had for five years."

"So back to Caudillo."

"He invited me to dinner on his yacht. We watched the sun set from one of his many decks and then he gave a toast to our sharing a long and fulfilling relationship. I sipped the wine. That's the last thing I remember. When I came to, the yacht was cruising across the Caribbean, and Misterioso Island had disappeared from sight."

"He kidnapped you?"

"And held me captive for ten horrifying months before I escaped to the Mexican mainland, changed my appearance and crossed the U.S. border under the radar, knowing it would be watched by Caudillo and his henchmen. You know the rest of the story."

Rage erupted inside Damien with a vehemence that sent adrenaline rushing though his veins. He hated to even imagine what this man had put her through while he held her captive.

Humiliation...torture...rape... His stomach clenched. "Where did he take you?"

"To his Caribbean-style mansion on his private island of Enmascarado, though parts of it were more like a fortress."

"From which he sold illegal arms," Damien said, quickly putting that part of the puzzle together. "Was he arming drug cartels?"

"I'm not sure who he did business with, but I can tell you that no matter how ruthless and evil his customers were, they can't compare to Caudillo."

And Emma had been with this psychopath for ten long months. A sick realization ground in his gut. "Is Belle Caudillo's daughter?"

Emma shook her head. "No, nor is she mine."

"Wait, you're not Belle's mother?"

"I told you this was complicated."

He listened as she told him about Belle's mother dying in the back of the truck and of how Emma had claimed to be her mother to save her life.

But his mind was still on Caudillo, and fury boiled inside Damien with the wrath of a wildfire.

"Did Caudillo or his henchmen hurt you?"

Emma stood and walked to the window. "I can't go there yet, Damien. One day soon, maybe, but not yet. I'm alive and I'm free of him. I want to stay that way."

And he wouldn't push that on her. "I understand."

"The main thing you need to understand is that Caudillo is a heartless, cold-blooded killer."

She pulled her arms tight across her chest and continued staring out the window as if the view could separate her from the images in her head.

"I saw him shoot a man in the head because he brought me food when Damien had ordered him not to."

Curses flew to Damien's lips before he could stop them. "Did he force you to have sex with him?"

"No." For the first time since she'd started talking, the muscles in her face relaxed. "The first time he tried, I got so sick I threw up in his face. He stomped away in disgust. Apparently splattering brains didn't faze him, but vomit turned him off forever. But only enough to keep from raping me. Sexual torment became his favorite game."

"That's over now. You're free of him."

"He'll never accept that. Caudillo is going to come looking for me, Damien, and you don't want to be in my life when he does. Even if I didn't know too much for him to let me live, he'd track me down and kill just to prove that no one betrays him and gets away with it. This is why you can't tell anyone about him and why you can't talk of my being kidnapped. Not even to your brothers."

"You're back in America, Emma. Go to the FBI. Tell them everything you've told me. They'll see that you're safe and that Caudillo is arrested."

"It's not that simple. Caudillo has connections in high places. He mentioned names of people in my office and told me things about them he wouldn't have known unless he had a source here. He even mentioned sources with the FBI."

"He could have been lying."

"I'm sure he wasn't lying when he told me that my disappearing was the media highlight of every cable news station for months. If I ever escaped and returned to the States, I'd be all over the news again. He'd track me easily and then he'd teach me the true meaning of torture."

"You can't hide from this man and his threats the rest of your life, Emma. And you can't let him continue to kidnap women at will."

"I don't plan to, but I have to have time to think this through, Damien. You don't know what it's like to live in captivity. You can't know how the fear eats at you when you never know if you'll be shot for merely asking for water."

She was right. He had no concept of that kind of fear. Emma was scared out of her wits but still worrying over an orphaned infant who had been pressed into her charge.

But once she walked away from Bent Pine Ranch, there was no one to watch over her.

He stepped closer. "I'll keep your secrets, Emma— under one condition."

"What is that?"

"You stay with me and let me protect you."

She buried her head in her hands. When she looked up, her eyes were moist. "You don't know how much I'd love to say yes to that offer."

"Then say it."

"I can't. I can't put you or your family in danger."

Damien walked over and took both her hands in his. "I won't put my family in danger, Emma, but I can't let you deal with this man on your own again. I have powerful connections, too, and resources that you don't. Let me help. At least stay a few days until we can locate Belle's father."

"That wouldn't be wise."

"It's the only sane thing to do. If you won't do it for you, do it for Belle."

"Are you sure?"

"Surer than I've ever been in my life."

"In that case, I don't see how I can refuse. I just hope you don't live to rue this day, Damien."

So did he. He wasn't worried about offering his help. That was a given. He wasn't convinced Caudillo would be crazy enough to come after her again. And as for his claims of connections in high places, those could be bogus, as well. Not that Damien wouldn't take all that into consideration. And he would make damn sure he kept his family safe.

But the biggest fear of the moment was that his libido was reacting too strongly to her, and that was the last thing she needed now.

Damien let go of her hands and stepped away. "Now we just have to decide how little we can tell the sheriff and still convince him you're innocent."

And how much he could tell his brothers without breaking his promise to Emma.

THE ENCLOSED BACK PORCH had been the family gathering spot for dealing with problems or celebrations for as long as Damien could remember. He stood there now, his hands buried deep in the pockets of his jeans, trying to assess the way Tague and Durk were reacting to the situation he'd just described for them.

Tague crossed an ankle over his knee. "So all the talk about getting lost while looking for her aunt's house was total fabrication?"

Damien nodded.

"Smuggling an orphaned illegal alien across the border was not smart," Durk said.

"Emma knows that now," Damien said, hating to have to lie to his brothers and getting the feeling they weren't really buying the lies anyway. Hopefully the sheriff would be less perceptive. Garcia frequently was.

Tague propped his feet on the coffee table. "So let me see if I have this right. Emma was living and working in Mexico. Her friend was dying and Emma promised her that she'd take her daughter to her American father in Dallas."

"That's basically it," Damien said. "Emma broke the law to help get Belle to her father. She paid some conniving son of a bitch to bring her across the border along with others he was hauling, and he tried to rape her."

"And now he conveniently ended up dead," Durk said.

"If that's the way you want to spin it. I've volunteered

to help Emma locate the baby's father and hire legal advice if the sheriff presses charges against her."

"And you're convinced she didn't kill the guy?" Tague asked.

"Totally convinced."

"Based on the fact she's been so honest with us up to now?" Durk quipped.

"Based on what she's admitted today and what I saw with my own eyes," Damien asserted. "She was running scared last night, the way someone would be if they'd just gotten away from a rapist."

"I get last night," Durk said. "Either one of us would have done the same as you. I'm just not convinced that hanging in there with her now is wise."

"Sorry you feel that way, Durk, because I plan to see her through this unless something happens to convince me I'm wrong about her innocence."

"How long do you plan to let her stay at the ranch?" Durk asked.

"As long as necessary. If that's a problem for either of you or for Mother, I'll take Emma and Belle to the hunting cabin or to a hotel in town."

"Sounds like you're committed to this," Tague said.

"I am."

"Then if it's fine with Mother, it won't bother me. I like Emma, and I can see why she'd want to do that for Belle."

Durk rubbed his chin, the same way Hugh used to do when he was giving one of his sons a lecture. "I think you know a whole lot more about Emma Smith—or whatever her real name is—than you're saying, Damien."

"I'm not denying that, but you're going to have to trust me and go along with me on this one."

"Is she in danger?" Durk asked.

"She could be, but not for anything that was her doing.

When I can tell you more, I will. In the meantime, I plan to make sure she's safe."

"A man has to do what he thinks is right, but be careful," Durk cautioned. "Check out all the facts for yourself. And try not to get personally involved. It wreaks havoc on objective judgment. And make damn sure you don't put Mother, Aunt Sybil or Grandma Pearl in any danger."

"Trust me on that. If we're square on this, I'll go check it out with Mother and make sure she's okay with Emma and Belle staying here in light of the sheriff's investigation."

"My guess is she'd keep that baby and give us away if it came to that," Tague joked. "One of us is going to have to give her grandkids one day soon. Keep in mind that I'm the youngest, so there's no pressure on me."

They talked a minute more about Julio's murder and then Damien left to go find Carolina. The mystery birth certificate started to nag at him again.

When faced with the task of taking responsibility for a dead stranger's infant girl, Emma apparently hadn't hesitated to jump right in.

What if Carolina's sister had left a helpless baby without anyone to care for it when she'd died? Damien had no doubt that his mother would have done the same as Emma.

But Carolina, with her faith and penchant for truth and doing what was right at all costs, would have never taken liberties with the truth. She'd have never created a fake birth certificate or claimed that Damien was her and Hugh's son if he wasn't. Would she?

He'd have to broach the subject of the birth certificate he'd found someday soon, but not today. His plate was not only full, it was spilling problems everywhere.

Once he talked to his mother, he'd have to get out of

the house. He always breathed and thought better in the saddle.

This time he'd take Emma along. After ten months of hell, she needed to get reacquainted with freedom, peace and a bit of tranquility before dealing with Sheriff Garcia. Hopefully the attorney he'd contacted would make dealing with the sheriff a little less stressful on Emma, as well.

As for Damien, he'd have to keep his growing attraction for Emma under control. After all, tropical islands weren't the only settings for romance in paradise.

Any cowboy in Texas could tell you that.

Chapter Six

They'd followed a winter wonderland trail that meandered along a riverbank before cutting through a thicket of pine trees. With each step of the gentle mare Damien had chosen for her, Emma felt her nerves starting to uncoil.

Not that she had any illusions that Caudillo was out of her life for good, but for the first time in what seemed forever, she didn't fear that he'd appear at any second. This world seemed totally removed from anything related to him.

Damien brought his horse to a halt and dismounted, looping the reins over the branch of a sycamore tree. "There's a lookout of sorts in that clearing ahead. It's worth the view if you'd like to stretch your legs for a few minutes."

"Sounds good."

His firm but gentle touch created a wellspring of awareness as he helped her slide from the saddle to the soft snow. She couldn't deny her growing attraction toward him, and the fact that she could react to his virility at all surprised her.

It might have been different if he'd made any demands on her, but Damien was nothing but gentle. Caudillo's torture had been psychological, the mental cruelty games at which he excelled. Damien, on the other hand, offered comfort and strength.

"I don't know how you knew, Damien, but this ride was exactly what I needed."

"It's what I do when I have problems to deal with."

She wondered if that was what he was doing now. Had he reconsidered after talking to his brothers and his mother and decided to renege on his offer of protection? If so, she certainly couldn't blame him. Still, prickles of anxiety began to jolt her temporary calm.

He took her hand as they climbed a rocky incline. "There's my life," he said, motioning to the pastoral scene that stretched out below them.

There were no mountains in this part of Texas, but still the view from the hilltop was impressive. Snow-covered pastures stretched out as far as she could see. There were also several barns, rows of fencing and cross-fencing and the sprawling house with its gables and chimneys and steep brown roof. And cattle. Hundreds of head of cattle.

"Is all of that the Bent Pine Ranch?"

"Not quite, but most. You can see some of Blake's spread from here, as well. That roofline you see in the distance just by the wooded area is his house."

"You are right. The view is awesome."

"It is from here. Down there, it's work, and lots of it. But running the ranch is what keeps me sane."

"I guess with a ranch like this you never had to think about what you wanted to be when you grew up."

"I went through the usual phases. Fireman. Astronaut. Bull rider."

"Bull rider? Seriously?"

"Yes, but after a few broken ribs, I figured there had to be a less painful way to make a living. By the time I was ready for college, I'd settled on ranching. Tague followed suit, and Durk went into the business side of Lambert Incorporated. We get the muscle aches, Durk gets the headaches."

"What is there to Lambert Inc. besides ranching?"

"Oil and natural gas."

That explained the wealth. "I think you got the better end of the deal. I love the openness of the ranch and the fact that it seems a million miles away from Caudillo."

"It is, Emma. That ordeal is behind you. You'll have difficult decisions to make about how to handle the events of the last ten months and how to make sure Caudillo doesn't kidnap other innocent women, but his control over you is finished."

She knew he believed that. "You're an amazing man, Damien Lambert."

"You know all the women in my life say that," he teased.

She figured the statement was truer than he'd actually admit to himself. It was a miracle she wandered onto his ranch, but the miracle would have a short shelf life. Till the sheriff released her and she located Belle's father.

Therein lay the next hurdle. Locating Juan Perez might take weeks or longer.

Only now that she thought about it, she didn't have to stick around until she located Juan, not if Carolina would agree to take up the baby's cause.

Carolina was great with Belle and loved taking care of her. That was clear from the way she'd jumped at the chance to watch her while Emma and Damien went horseback riding. And Carolina had wealth and influence, everything needed to conduct a search for Belle's father. All Emma had was determination.

Emma wouldn't bring it up with Damien, but she'd start laying the groundwork with Carolina. It was the perfect solution for letting her clear out of Damien's life before he tired of her and kicked her out. And before Caudillo tracked her down.

They lingered at the lookout a few more minutes before climbing into the saddles for the ride back to the ranch house.

When they arrived, there were two cars in the driveway that hadn't been there before. One was a red Porsche. The other was the sheriff's squad car.

"Looks like the sheriff has arrived," Damien said.

"What about the other car?"

"That would be Cletus Markham. He's an attorney who'll be on hand when you talk to the sheriff."

"A criminal defense attorney who makes house calls on Saturday at the spur of the moment?"

"Actually, he's a corporate lawyer on retainer by Lambert Inc., but he'll be able to handle a simple interrogation. We'll upgrade to a criminal defense attorney if it becomes necessary, but I doubt that it will."

"I can't afford a lawyer."

"No problem. Like I said, Cletus is on retainer."

"It's a problem for me. I don't like the idea of being one of your charity cases, Damien."

"You're not. You can pay me back one day when you get your life in order. But a man's dead and you were likely the last person to see him alive. You need an attorney."

"Attorneys. Vets. Even the sheriff. Is there anything you can't get via home delivery with a phone call, Damien?"

"Rain, good beef prices and an honest politician, but I'm working on that last one."

Perhaps she'd underestimated Damien Lambert. Maybe he was a match for Caudillo after all.

But was she a match for Sheriff Garcia? She was about to get her chance to find out.

EMMA'S FIRST UP CLOSE AND personal impression of Sheriff Garcia was that he didn't like murders messing up his Saturdays. It took only a few minutes to extend that to the assumption that he didn't like her.

She was the outsider who was causing the problem. When he acknowledged her, he glared as if she were an affront to the good people of his county.

"We can talk in Dad's old study," Damien said.

Emma, Sheriff Garcia and the attorney followed Damien down the hallway to the same room where Damien had stripped away the bloody wrap last night. Today, the room crackled with tension and the sheriff's unfriendly vibes.

Emma settled in the same chair she'd sat in last night. Damien dragged a reading chair from the opposite corner and pulled it over to sit next to her. Making it known whose side he was on, she thought.

He wouldn't have chosen hers had she not leveled with him about Caudillo. Hopefully the sheriff was not as good at seeing through her lies as Damien had been.

Sheriff Garcia waved off Damien's offer of the black leather swivel chair and instead decided to prop his backside on the edge of the desk. A power position, she guessed, though as far as she was concerned his title of Sheriff provided that.

Cletus Markham rolled the leather chair into a position that let him face either the sheriff or Emma with a turn of his head.

Cletus made her more uneasy than the sheriff did. He was somewhere in the mid-fifties with gray, thinning hair and a body that suggested he made regular trips to the gym. He wore an expensive blue suit, a stiff-collared maroon shirt and a silk tie a shade or two darker than the shirt.

His formality set him apart from the jeans, sweater and Western boots Damien wore and even further apart from her in the slightly baggy jeans and loose-fitting sweater Carolina had let her borrow for the day.

The sheriff took her personal information, name, date of birth and address.

"So you live in Mexico?"

"I did. I don't plan to return."

"Don't blame you for getting out," Garcia said. "It's getting dangerous down there, what with the drug cartels taking over. What took you there in the first place?"

"A relationship, but it ended months ago."

The sheriff scratched behind his right ear and stared at the bandage on her arm. "What happened to your arm?"

"Julio tried to rape me. I fought him off and he swung a knife. It sliced my arm."

"Julio?"

"The man who was found dead this morning. He drove the truck that smuggled me and many others across the border."

Damien said almost nothing during the rest of the interrogation, but Cletus Markham made sure he earned his fee. He objected so many times, it was difficult for Emma to get her prearranged story out.

Finally, she interrupted the attorney. "I don't have anything to hide. I didn't kill Julio. The knife was never in my hands. Even if it had been, I would have been no match for him. I had Belle cradled in my rebozo and Julio was twice my size."

"Was there anyone else in the truck or the trailer when the alleged rape attempt took place?" the sheriff asked.

"I've already told you that he kept me locked in the trailer after releasing the others. He drove for about fifteen minutes and then stopped again. That's when he attacked me, and I resent the word *alleged* being used."

"Ask your questions," Cletus protested, "and stop trying to put words into my client's mouth."

The sheriff stared at Damien. "Does this joker have to be here?"

"He's Emma's attorney, so he has every right," Damien countered.

This was fast becoming a circus.

"You say you didn't have a knife, but you were engaged in a fight?" the sheriff said, rephrasing a question he'd already asked in a dozen different ways.

"I told you. He tried to rape me. I tried to stop him. We struggled and I finally got in one good kick that buckled his knees and took him down. I took off running and got away from the truck as fast as I could."

"And when he went down, you think it's possible that he fell on his knife."

"We established that fact twenty minutes ago," Cletus said.

"Where is this baby that you smuggled into the country now?"

"Mother's watching her," Damien answered. "And I can vouch for part of Emma's story. I found her bleeding, freezing and cradling Belle on my spread out near Beaver Creek. All she asked for was shelter and food for the baby. Blake Benson came over and stitched up the arm."

No mention of the aunt or the ditched car. It would only confuse the issue, Damien had suggested to her earlier.

Sheriff Garcia patted the pocket of his khaki uniform shirt as if feeling for a pack of cigarettes. Habit, no doubt. The pocket was empty.

"So let's see if I have this clear, Emma," the sheriff said.

"You're claiming accidental death while trying to defend yourself?"

"She's told you what happened," Cletus said. "Emma knows she made a mistake by smuggling Belle across the border, but she's an American citizen who was being attacked. She had every right to defend herself."

"The investigation is far from over," the sheriff said. "I'm running fingerprints and DNA testing on the victim and the knife. It's likely he has a record in the U.S. If he does, that will give us positive identification."

"Then you're not pressing any kind of charges against my client?" Cletus asked.

"That all depends."

"On what?" Damien asked.

"Whether or not you want to take on the responsibility of seeing that she doesn't flee. There aren't many men I'd trust that way, but everyone in these parts knows that a Lambert is as good as his word."

"I'm willing," Damien said. "She can stay at the ranch and I'll make certain she doesn't leave the house unless I'm with her. Or unless one of my brothers is accompanying her."

Cletus jumped to his feet. "I think we need to talk about this."

"No need," Damien said. "The decision is made."

The sheriff crossed the room and stopped near Emma's chair. His cold stare seemed to penetrate her skull.

"Even if Julio's death was self-defense, if I find out that you were involved in the human-trafficking operation, I'll do whatever I can to see that you get everything the law can throw at you. Is that clear?"

"Yes, sir, and I would deserve it."

"Now, what do you plan to do with that baby?"

"I'll hire a private investigator to find the father," Damien said.

"You realize I'll have to notify Child Protective Services. They'll investigate and handle this as they see fit."

"Do what you have to," Damien said. "But assure them she's being well cared for."

"I also have to notify the U.S. Immigration and Customs Enforcement agency," Garcia said. "Of course, with the backlog ICE has, Belle may be in college before they get around to checking it out, unless this Juan Perez is an illegal with a criminal record."

"Is that all?" Damien asked.

"That and the fact that the investigation into the victim's death will be ongoing. If I want to get in touch with Emma, I expect her to be available, Damien."

"You can reach me at my cell number twenty-four hours a day."

"Then it's settled. Emma, you can be exceedingly grateful that you were found by a Lambert."

"I am."

But the poisonous anger toward Caudillo was swelling inside her again. He'd reduced her to lies and schemes and fear that kept her from using her own name or reclaiming her life.

He'd robbed her of the person she was inside and left her a shell of the person she'd been.

She lost track of the conversation until Damien took her arm and his touch nudged her back into the present.

"Thanks," she whispered as they walked the sheriff to the door.

"Hang in there, Emma. This will all work out."

Easy for him to say. He didn't know Caudillo...*yet*.

RELIEVED THAT THINGS HAD gone so well with the sheriff, Damien rejoined Cletus in the study. Cletus jumped up from his chair and closed the door. "What the hell were you thinking, Damien?"

Cletus's reaction didn't surprise him, but it did irritate him. "I'm helping out a woman in trouble. What part of that do you have a problem with?"

"How about the part where you just agreed to be responsible for a woman you know nothing about?"

"I know enough to believe she didn't kill this Julio guy."

"And how do you know that? Because she said it? Because she made gooey, innocent eyes at you? Because you have the hots for her?"

"I don't make decisions based on hots, or colds, either, for that matter."

"Or good sense, apparently. Did it cross your mind that the baby's mother might not be dead? Emma Smith—not likely her real name—may be one of those women who can't have children and doesn't meet adoption criteria."

"What's your point?" Damien asked.

"She could have bought that baby on the black market. Then smuggling the infant into the U.S. makes sense. Believe me, that happens a lot more often than you think, though most find a safer way of getting back into the States."

"She didn't buy the baby."

"Then how about the fact that for all we know she was the victim's accomplice? Or she might be wanted by the law here and had to keep a low profile when crossing the border? There is any number of scenarios to explain why she'd be on that truck, none of them pretty."

And none as bizarre as the story of the kidnapping. Yet Damien was convinced that Emma was telling the truth about Caudillo. If he was wrong about that, he'd never be able to trust his instincts again.

"Bottom line," Cletus said, "is that you don't need to be sticking your neck out for that woman."

"That's my decision to make."

"Have you talked to Carolina and your brothers about her staying here?"

"I have, and they're good with it."

"If your father were here, he wouldn't be."

"I'm not so sure about that. Dad was the first to lend a hand when someone needed help."

"He was always there when a *friend* needed help," Cletus argued. "Emma Smith doesn't fall into that category. Hugh was passionate about a lot of things, but he always got his facts straight before he made decisions. You'd be wise to do the same."

Damien agreed. That's why even though he trusted Emma, he was having Caudillo investigated. Quietly. Covertly. By a man he knew he could trust. He saw no reason to discuss that with Cletus.

"I appreciate your coming out today, Cletus. I know it was short notice and the roads are not in the best of shape."

"They're fine now, but the temperature is dropping down into the low twenties tonight, so by dark those bridges and overpasses will start icing up again."

Cletus stuck out his hand. The handshake, signifying the discussion had finished, was firm and friendly in spite of their differences of opinion.

"Just be careful, Damien. This woman could be trouble."

Cletus didn't know the half of it.

CAROLINA STOOD AT THE oversize range and stirred the rich chocolaty mixture. The fragrant odor of snickerdoodle cookies baking in the oven filled the room.

Nothing like cookies and hot cocoa on a snowy afternoon.

The last time they'd had a good ground cover of snow was three years ago—when Hugh was still alive. She remembered it vividly. Hugh had insisted she go four-wheeling with him. They'd ridden all the way out to the north property line.

She'd made snow angels. He'd laughed and teased her about still being a kid. After he'd helped brush the snow from her backside, he'd pulled her into his arms and kissed her hard. She'd felt as giddy as a schoolgirl.

She'd been crazy in love with Hugh from the day she met him. And even though they'd had their disagreements over the years, she was still in love with him. People kept telling her that time would ease the pain of losing him. Perhaps it would, but she hoped the memories never dimmed.

When the chocolate was hot, she moved it off the flame and checked the cookies. They were golden-brown.

She'd baked a lot more frequently when the boys were young. Now she stayed far too busy with her church and charity work—attempts to keep her from constantly grieving for Hugh. But she still loved lazy afternoons in her kitchen, especially when the whole family was around.

Hugh had called their old, marred kitchen table the heart of the family. It still was, she guessed, though without Hugh it seemed part of the heart was missing.

"Whatever you're cooking smells divine."

Carolina set the sheet of cookies on two hot pads and turned to respond to Emma. "Snickerdoodles and cocoa. Are you up for a break?"

"I am now that my mouth is watering."

"Sit down at the table and I'll pour us a cup of the hot chocolate."

"I'll get a plate for the cookies and some napkins," Emma said.

"Just like a tea party," Carolina said.

It amazed her how quickly she'd bonded with Emma. Actually, the news that Belle wasn't her daughter hadn't surprised Carolina in the least. She was much too awkward with Belle for the baby to be her child.

But Emma was loving and gentle with the infant, and that made up for any uneasiness she had handling Belle.

"I'm glad you shed that black wig," Carolina said. "Your natural hair is so becoming."

"Thanks. I was trying to blend in with the others who were being smuggled across the border."

"Bringing Belle to her father was a very commendable and humane thing to do."

"As was your taking us both in."

"Like I told you, you and Belle are a blessing."

"Actually, I need to ask another favor," Emma said, "but feel free to say no if you're busy."

Carolina settled in a chair kitty-cornered from Emma. "What's the favor?"

"Damien insists that he drive me to the closest urgent-care center just to have them take a look at my arm. I assured him it's not necessary, but he says Blake recommended I get it checked out again today."

"And you'd like me to watch Belle for you?"

"If you would. She's asleep now, but she'll probably wake for her bottle soon. I'd rather not take her around sick people who could have something contagious. She's so tiny. I can't bear to think of her getting ill."

"I'll be glad to watch her. In fact, I can think of no better way to spend the rest of the afternoon."

"Hopefully, we won't be gone too long."

"You never know about those places, but don't worry

if it takes longer than expected. On the way home, have Damien stop at the pharmacy and pick up some more formula and diapers."

"I will, and some more disposable liners for the bottles. Those work well." Emma nibbled at her cookie. "There is one more thing I'd like to ask you about, and I'd really appreciate a truthful answer."

"You'll always get that from me, though I may lace my words with tact."

"How do you really feel about my staying on here while the sheriff finishes his investigation? I know the situation is difficult, and if you'd rather I leave, I'll go."

Carolina trailed her fingers along the handle of her mug. "If you weren't going to stay here, the sheriff would likely have arrested you. Jail is no place for Belle."

"Belle wouldn't have to go with me, not if you offered to look after her until her biological father is found or until I'm fully cleared and free to leave the area."

The comment caught Carolina off guard and aroused her suspicions. "Why do I have the feeling there is something you're not telling me?"

"It's not that," Emma said quickly. "I just don't want to be here if you're not comfortable with having me in the house."

But Carolina was almost certain there was more behind the suggestion that she take responsibility for Belle. She loved having Belle around, but she wasn't sure how she'd feel about taking care of her day after day, only to give her up to a stranger that she might not even like.

Emma might have those same fears, perhaps unconsciously. She certainly seemed to be attached to the infant.

"I like having both you and Belle here, Emma. Now go and get your wound checked out."

Emma would make a wonderful mother one day. And

with her ready smile, her ability to deal with problems and her graciousness, she'd make a fantastic wife. Carolina hoped Damien was taking serious note of that.

Unless Emma was fooling them all.

THE DOCTOR ON DUTY AT THE urgent-care facility had assured Emma that her arm was healing fine and recommended she have the stitches taken out in five days. After that, they'd made a quick stop at a Walmart, where Emma had stocked up on supplies for Belle and picked up some personal items for herself.

The rest of the afternoon and evening passed without incident, though Emma had seen little of Damien since returning to the house. Other than coming to the table for dinner, he'd remained hidden away somewhere in the house. She didn't know if he was avoiding her or researching Caudillo. Either way, she worried.

Durk had spent most of the time on the enclosed porch, pouring over legal documents and talking on the phone.

Tague, however, had made sure Emma was not neglected. He'd taken her with him to feed the horses and then fascinated her with stories about growing up on the ranch. He'd even asked to hold Belle, but he gave her back quickly when the smells coming from her diaper indicated poop duty. Emma had made quick work of remedying that.

"You smell like a baby now, though, don't you, little sweetie?" Emma crooned as she lifted Belle to her shoulder for a burp.

When that was taken care of, she lay Belle in her beautiful antique cradle and rocked her gently. Belle's eyes closed and in seconds she drifted off to sleep.

"Sweet dreams, my precious. Your mother loved you very much, Belle," she whispered. "I hope your father makes sure you know that." But fathers had a way of forgetting little girls exist, at least that was how it had been in her world.

Emma placed a kiss on Belle's forehead and then dropped onto her bed, lying in the darkness as the events of the past two days skirted through her mind like slippery ghosts. She'd planned and plotted her eventual escape from the first minute she realized she'd been kidnapped. Never once did she imagine a man like Damien dropping into her life. Now that he had, she had no idea how to handle her feelings for him.

It was after two in the morning before she finally fell into a restless sleep.

She woke to the sound of her bedroom door creaking open. She opened her eyes and sat up in bed as her eyes slowly adjusted to the darkness and the shadows creeping across the walls.

"Damien?"

"Yes. I've brought him to you, my beloved Emma."

The voice was Caudillo's. Dread cut off the blood supply to her brain, leaving her nauseous and dizzy.

"Where do you want this?"

Finally her eyes focused on the bloody head that rested in Caudillo's hand.

Chapter Seven

Damien jerked awake to the bloodcurdling scream. Not bothering to pull on his jeans, he raced down the hallway, shoved open the door and burst into the guest room.

Emma was sitting up in bed, shaking so hard her teeth were rattling. Belle started to cry. Lights popped on throughout the house. Footfalls sounded from all directions.

Damien walked to the edge of the bed. "Are you okay? What happened?"

Emma jumped from the bed and picked up Belle, rocking her in her arms to console the startled infant.

"I had this nightmare, only it was so real. Caudillo was standing by the door holding…" Her voice broke so that she couldn't finish the sentence.

"We heard screams," Tague said from the doorway behind Damien.

"What's wrong?" Durk asked.

Carolina pushed around them and into the room. "Is it Belle?"

"Belle's fine. It was just a nightmare. I'm sorry I woke all of you."

"I'm not surprised at the bad dream," Carolina said, "not after what you've been through. Do you want me to take Belle?"

"No, really, I'm fine. And Belle has already stopped crying. Please, just go back to sleep. I feel bad enough that I woke you."

"I second that," Damien said. "All of you go back to bed. I'll handle things from here."

It wasn't until they'd all left that he realized how presumptuous he'd sounded. Worse, he was standing in Emma's bedroom in his boxers and her in the cotton nightshirt she'd picked up when he'd taken her shopping that afternoon.

He expected Emma to kick him out, as well. When she didn't he dropped to the edge of the bed and watched her pace the room, rocking Belle in her arms.

"Are you really okay?" he asked.

"Not so much," she admitted.

"Do you want to talk about it?"

She didn't answer.

"I'm wide-awake now, and I'm a good listener."

"How many nightmares do you want to hear about? Tonight's or ten months' worth?"

"As much as you feel like sharing."

She placed Belle back in the cradle and sat on the opposite side of the bed from him. She rocked the cradle with one hand, turning so that she could look at him in the glow of moonlight that filtered through the windowpanes.

"There were lots of times over the last ten months when I feared Caudillo would drive me to the edge of madness. Tonight I thought he had."

"I could hear that in your scream."

"So you came running but stayed calm and in control. How did you ever learn so much about handling hysterical women?"

"I wouldn't call you hysterical. In fact, you're exceptionally levelheaded for a woman who's been through ten months of captivity. You've even reached out to Belle and have become a lifesaver to her."

"It's more like we saved each other."

When the rhythmic sounds of Belle's breathing indicated she'd fallen back asleep, Emma propped her pillows against the headboard and scooted until her back pressed against them. She pulled the sheet up to her waist.

"You may as well get comfortable, too, Damien. Since you volunteered, this could turn into a long therapy session."

Being in bed with Emma might be a lot of things, but he doubted comfortable was going to be one of them.

FIVE DAYS AGO, WHEN EMMA had tasted her first sweet breath of freedom, she'd fully expected to never share the horrid story of her months with Caudillo with another living soul. All she wanted was to push it to the deepest depths of her consciousness.

Any eventual communication with law enforcement would have been carried out anonymously, as if she were on the outside looking in. And that only after she felt safe.

Weirdly, from almost the first moment she'd met Damien Lambert, she'd felt the urge to let the details pour from her heart and her mouth. It made no sense.

Like Caudillo, Damien was wealthy and no doubt had an impressive realm of influence. But where Caudillo had faked a suave and cosmopolitan attitude, Damien was the real thing: rugged, with the swagger of a cowboy, the confidence of a man firmly fixed in his values and the manners of a gentleman.

And unbelievably protective. She'd expected it to be years before she felt at ease with a man. Now she was lying in bed with Damien and ready to open up.

She raised her arms and slid her hands behind her head.

"One of the weirdest initial things about the kidnapping was that Caudillo seemed surprised that I was upset. He said I should have realized as he did that we were meant to be together, and that he was just making it easy for me."

"So he was mentally deranged as well as evil."

"Some of the time he seemed to be. At other times, he seemed exceptionally rational, like when he insisted I give him access to the files of specific agents in our field office."

"Did you?"

"I couldn't have if I wanted to, but for some reason he was convinced I was lying about that."

"Was he trying to get specific information or just fishing for information to help him avoid getting caught in their web?"

"I was never sure. Caudillo prided himself on answering to no man—and definitely not to a woman."

"Did he let you use the internet?"

"Never. The only time I was ever allowed to leave my quarters was when he was with me. As he reminded me often, I was completely at his mercy. My life existed for his pleasure and purposes."

"What were your living quarters like?"

"Elegant, as if I were a guest in his mansion. The closet was filled with revealing gowns that looked like something whores in the Middle Ages might have worn. Caudillo brought them back from his many trips. He presented them like they were valuable gifts. Bras and panties were not to be worn at all when he was in the house.

"The bathroom was stocked with bath oils and perfumes and baskets of makeup that I was expected to wear every day in case he decided to pay me a visit."

"And if you didn't?"

"Then I participated in a forced period of fasting, usually lasting at least three days, to cleanse my heart and body."

"But he never touched you sexually?"

Emma sucked in her breath as the images infiltrated her mind. Even thousands of miles away from him, she grew nauseous.

"You don't have to answer that," Damien said, evidently sensing her growing discomfort.

But saying it out loud would hopefully dispel some of the power it held over her. "Like I told you, we never had sex. He claimed he was withholding it from me due to his disgust at my unseemly reaction to his first attempt. Who knew vomit could be such a blessing?"

"But he did touch you?"

"He made me sit on his lap while he told me what he referred to as 'stories' to make me understand him."

Damien rolled his eyes.

"Exactly, as if I didn't already understand more about him than I ever wanted to know."

She hesitated again. The rest of what she had to say was the torturous part, the words that had fueled a hundred nightmares almost as gruesome as tonight's.

"The stories always began with his childhood. The beatings he received at the hands of his father. The cruel and inhumane treatment from his stepmother. The nights he'd plotted killing them both, always culminating with the way he'd eventually cut their hearts from their chests and fed them to their dogs before disposing of their mangled bodies."

"Did you believe him?"

"I did. The distortions in his face said it all. But he didn't stop there. He went on to tell me about other women he'd kidnapped, though he never used that word. He spoke of them as guests. He'd tell me how he pampered them but it was never enough, so eventually he'd had to kill them. He didn't spare the details of those murders, either."

"Proof that you were being held by a psychopath and insurance that you'd obey his every order."

"I'm sure that was his purpose. Instead it only made me more determined than ever to get away from him."

"How many women were there when you escaped?"

"Just me."

"And when you arrived?"

"There were three of us. The first one disappeared almost immediately. Caudillo told me she'd drowned while trying to escape. I only saw the second woman a couple of times. She seemed sickly, pale and anorexic thin. I think he may have literally starved her to death."

"Thank God you escaped."

"It was only by chance."

"How did it happen?"

"Caudillo was away from the island. I heard gunfire, and the noise that followed suggested chaos. I screamed. An armed man that I'd never seen before burst through my door, glanced my way and then left. When I peeked out the door I realized that the fortress had been overrun with gunmen and that the usual guards were nowhere in sight.

"I walked out of my room but then ducked into Caudillo's office when I heard more gunfire. His safe had been ransacked. Hundred-dollar bills the raiders must have dropped littered the floor. I grabbed what I could and then ran to the beach and waited for the opportunity to board the boat that the gunmen had come in on."

"Were they stealing weapons as well as money?"

"Yes, huge crates of them. When I saw my chance I boarded and hid in the galley behind the crates. The boat left the island shortly after I boarded."

"Left for where?"

"Mexico. I escaped the next morning while the thieves celebrated their victory."

"You're one spunky woman, Emma Smith. You may still have some hard days in front of you, but you'll get through this and come out just fine."

"You're far more convinced of that than I am, cowboy." Keeping the rest of the truth from him seemed a violation of trust. "Now that I've told you this much, I may as well clear up another of my lies."

"There's more?"

"Afraid so. My real name is Emma Muran. Now you know all there is to know, but I still hold you to your promise not to reveal my identity or my connection to Caudillo."

Damien put an arm around her shoulders and pulled her into the curl of his arm. "He's not going to kill you, Emma, not as long as I have your back. Now why don't you relax and get some sleep before Belle wakes up again, ready to eat."

She knew it was false assurance, but Emma let it embrace her like silk. She closed her eyes and fell asleep, still sheltered in Damien's arms.

THE SUN HAD BARELY KISSED the horizon when Damien pulled on his jacket and stepped out the back door. His breath quickly turned to vapor in the cold air. He hurried down the steps, slid behind the wheel of his pickup and revved the motor.

It was less than a quarter of a mile to the ranch offices. Usually he walked it to get his blood pumping and his mind focused on the duties of the day, but today he was eager to see if Carson Stile had faxed him anything on Caudillo overnight.

Damien had met Carson during his senior year at A&M. They'd shared a statistics class and been teamed by the teacher to work on a project. Damien figured the teacher had thought of it as an academia-type joke. The rich rancher's kid, who liked sports and dabbled in rodeo, paired with the California scholarship nerd, who spent most of his time playing video games in his room or hanging out in the computer lab.

Oddly, they'd hit it off, and when Carson lost his scholarship due to funding cutbacks, Hugh had picked up the tab. Hugh hadn't really expected to see the money again, but Carson had paid back every cent.

He was working for a tech company in Seattle now. Not surprising, since Damien knew for a fact there hadn't been a file in the A&M system Carson couldn't have hacked into. But for the most part, Carson played it straight. He did, however, have the full scoop on every professor on staff.

The last time Damien had seen Carson was two years ago, when Carson had been in Dallas for a conference. He'd driven out and spent a week at the ranch when it concluded. Carson had diligently avoided everything on four legs, especially the bulls.

The second Damien opened the door at the ranch headquarters, he knew he'd made the right decision in calling Carson last night. The fax machine was stacked with new pages. Carson had obviously kept company with his computer until late into the night.

Damien started a pot of coffee, picked up the faxed pages and started reading the scoop on Anton Klein, better known in the Caribbean as Caudillo.

It read more like a legend or a fairy tale than pure facts. Damien spent the next hour absorbing the information and trying to get an accurate assessment of the bastard who'd ripped Emma's life apart.

A billionaire playboy who had several residences in Europe, including a castle in Ireland, an opulent villa in France, a vineyard in Italy and, of course, a tropical island in the Caribbean. The island was said to be his retreat, and few people had ever been invited onto the premises.

At almost two hundred feet in length, his craft was one of the largest privately owned vessels in the world. Many friends and acquaintances and even European and Middle East royalty had apparently spent time with him on his yacht.

Caudillo was said to be charming, handsome, generous and exceedingly mysterious. Although he came from a family of successful shipping magnates, that didn't fully explain his vast wealth.

Speculation about that ran from involvement in the blood diamond trade to involvement with corrupt dictators. Oddly, there was no mention of illegal arms, even though he was known by a name meaning "warlord."

There were vague references to his being a man you wouldn't want to cross. Damien had to wonder if that was because those who had crossed him were no longer breathing.

Nothing directly contradicted Emma's description of him, yet nothing painted him as the kind of twisted psychopath she'd described.

But seeing Emma's anguish over the past two days, he was convinced that Caudillo was exactly as she'd described him.

Caudillo had to be stopped before another female became his victim. Damien just wasn't sure of the best way to go about that yet.

An hour and two cups of coffee later, a plan of action

was forming in Damien's mind. He'd read enough about Caudillo. But there was one search he'd have to do himself, at least until Emma released him from his promise not to reveal her true identity.

Telling him her real name had been a giant leap of faith. He wouldn't betray her—unless her safety depended on it.

But he would not let Caudillo near her again. In his mind, that more than justified what he had to do next.

He could remember several well-publicized disappearances in recent years, but he had no recollection of an American woman disappearing while vacationing in the Caribbean ten months ago. If it had been covered up, he intended to find out why and by whom.

He typed "Emma Muran" in his search engine. Several subjects came up. An artist in Toronto. A musician in New Orleans. A gourmet caterer in Phoenix. There was no mention of an Emma Muran who'd disappeared while vacationing in paradise.

He kept searching and finally uncovered where Emma had gone to high school and the academic honors she'd earned while attending the University of Alabama. He even found her address and phone number in Nashville. There was absolutely nothing about a kidnapping.

But surely her family would have reported her as missing. If not, then the friend who was supposed to go with her would have gone to the police.

Something was seriously wrong with this picture.

He killed the screen and pulled his cell phone from his pocket. It was time to set the plan in action. But he wouldn't do it behind Emma's back.

EMMA SPOONED A BITE OF creamy yogurt into her mouth and swallowed without tasting, oblivious to the family chatter around the table.

Damien's absence at the breakfast table created a sense of foreboding in Emma that bordered on panic. He'd seen her at her most vulnerable last night. Had she seemed too needy? Was he reconsidering his efforts to help her find Belle's father and to escape arrest?

If he had, she couldn't blame him. Yet, even though she'd begged him yesterday to let her walk away, thinking he was ready to abandon her now created immense apprehension.

If the sheriff booked her and checked her fingerprints, he could quickly ascertain her identity. Everyone who worked for the ATF had their fingerprints in the database.

The records would show that she'd been kidnapped. Supplying the media with her name and location was tantamount to drawing Caudillo a map straight to her.

But the thought of Damien's abandoning her went deeper. It seemed to cut to her very soul. She had bared it all last night. Rejection now was a rejection of her as a person.

"How about some of this raspberry jam for your toast, Emma? A friend who owns a quaint teahouse in Dallas makes it, and it's delicious."

Carolina's offer pulled her back into the moment. "In that case, I should definitely try some."

"I hope you don't mind a light breakfast," Carolina said as she passed the jam. "It's become a tradition around here on Sunday, since I teach a Sunday School class and have to be at the church quite early."

"No complaints from me," Emma said. "Yogurt, fruit, cereal, toast, juice. All my favorites."

"I play the organ for the service," Sybil said, making sure she wasn't outdone by Carolina. "I've missed less than a dozen times in the past ten years. And that's with this bad hip."

"That's very impressive," Emma said. "I'd love to hear you play sometime."

"She plays too loud," Pearl said. "Makes my hearing aids vibrate."

Sybil rolled her eyes at her mother's comment. "No one else complains about the volume. At least I use my talents for God."

"So do I," Pearl added with a sly smile and the familiar mischievous twinkle in her wrinkle-rimmed eyes. "I'm the reverend's clock watcher. I sit in the second pew, where he can't miss me. I start tapping my watch when it nears noon. I've told him if he can't get it said by twelve, then save it for next week."

"And that's the uncondensed version of why we're forced to starve on Sunday mornings," Tague joked as he retrieved the coffeemaker from the counter and refilled the empty cups.

Carolina wiped her mouth on her napkin. "You've never gone hungry in your life, Tague Lambert."

"Except on Sunday mornings," Durk said, joining the teasing. "By the way, does anyone know what Damien is up to this morning? I took an early-morning ride on Ranger and noticed his truck parked at headquarters. He's working kind of early for a Sunday morning."

"He's speaking to the Cattlemen's Association tomorrow night," Tague said. "He's probably working on the speech."

Carolina stood and started clearing the table. "He has a lot on his mind. Maybe he just needed some time alone."

Pearl entertained them through the remainder of the meal with stories from the past. The rest of the family had likely heard them a million times before, but they all laughed and joined in as if they were hearing them for the first time.

The Lamberts were an amazing family—which only added guilt to Emma's growing angst about drawing them into danger.

"So who's on the schedule for supper tonight?" Durk asked.

"No one." Carolina stood and started gathering dishes. "The Huberts and the Gaylords were supposed to drive out from Dallas, but we decided to postpone for a week due to weather conditions. Of course, I didn't realize then that the temperature was going to climb back into the fifties today."

"Having friends and neighbors over for Sunday suppers at the Bent Pine Ranch is another tradition," Tague explained to Emma. "Only with that one you get real food."

"I need to make a few calls," Durk said, "but let me know when you're ready and I'll drive you to church. The roads may still be icy in spots."

"Aren't you going with us?" Sybil asked.

"Not this morning."

"Yeah, count me out, too," Tague said.

"What are you two up to?" Carolina asked.

"Damien called a meeting. He said for right after breakfast, but since he hasn't shown up, he may have forgotten about it."

"He didn't mention a meeting to me," Carolina said.

Durk shook his head. "I don't think it's company related."

"He's probably planning a hunting trip," Tague said. "Grandma, you should go hunting with us."

"I might just do that, young man."

Everyone laughed except Emma. Her mind remained on the upcoming meeting and the fear that it had to do with her. She stood and gathered the rest of the dishes. "Let me finish up in the kitchen for you, Mrs. Lambert."

"Sunday dishes are my job," Sybil said, "and it won't take me but a jiffy. Why don't you go and take a few minutes for yourself before Belle wakes up."

"She's sleeping awfully late this morning," Carolina said. "Are you sure she's okay?"

"Actually she started her day before any of us. She was up at six for a bottle and drained it dry. She's napping now, but I left the door open so I'll hear her if she cries."

Emma began to put away the jams and butter.

"We'd love to have you and Belle join us for church if you're interested," Carolina said. "I have a pair of dress slacks and a blouse that should fit better than the jeans and sweater I gave you yesterday. They're a little tight on me."

"Thanks for the invitation, but not today," Emma said. Fortunately, Damien walked in the back door before she had to explain further.

"You missed breakfast," Pearl said, her tone playfully scolding.

Damien raked his fingers through his hair, but the attempt to smooth the dark, thick locks failed. Instead it left him looking devilishly rakish, and her traitorous pulse spiked. It should be impossible to worry that he'd betrayed her and still feel sensual awareness.

"No problem about breakfast," Damien said. "I'll grab something later. Right now I have something to discuss with Emma."

"Guess that's our signal to clear out," Tague said.

"No, you guys finish your coffee. Emma and I can talk on the porch and then I'll get back with you."

"I just offered to help with cleanup chores," Emma said.

"The dishes can wait."

Whatever was on his mind was serious. Her insides quaked a little as she followed him to the porch.

"So is this where the cowboy rides away?" she asked,

trying for nonchalance but hearing a shaky quiver in her voice.

His eyebrows arched. "If you mean that the way it sounds, then the answer is a resounding no. I told you I'd see you through this. I don't go back on my word, Emma. Not unless I find out you're plying me with more lies."

"Everything I told you last night was the truth."

"Good. Now I need you to tell me more about Enmascarado Island."

"Like what?"

"The layout of the house, docks, outbuildings and any other structures you noted while you were there."

"Why?"

"Because I'm flying to Miami tonight and on to Enmascarado first thing tomorrow morning."

Chapter Eight

Emma dropped into one of the rockers, temporarily shocked speechless by Damien's unexpected announcement.

"Tell me I heard you wrong," she said when her brain stopped even trying to process the ridiculous statement.

"You heard me right. He has to be stopped. It's going to take proof of his breaking the law to do that."

"And I suppose you think you're going to single-handedly fly down there, snoop around beneath the nose of one of the most evil men alive, get your proof and walk away from that island alive."

"Now, that would make a great Rambo movie. But that's not what I had in mind."

"What do you have in mind, Damien? Because this sounds like a suicide mission to me."

"Rest assured it isn't. I'll do a couple of flybys to scope out the place."

"Why can't you just let me handle this my way, Damien?"

"Refresh my memory on that plan."

"Once I'm settled, I'll send anonymous messages to the ATF, the CIA and the FBI. They'll check it out and go after Caudillo. They have the manpower to do it."

"Right, and anonymous messages always go right to the top of their priority list. And if they do check him out, they may not even discover that he deals in illegal arms, much less that he kidnaps and tortures innocent women."

"Why do you always have to make so much sense?"

"You'd come to the same conclusions if the bastard hadn't done such a number on you."

Her nerves jumped into panic mode. "I knew this would happen, Damien. I knew from the first that telling you the truth would eventually put you in harm's way."

"I won't be in danger, Emma. It's just a flight. Even Caudillo doesn't shoot down planes flying over his island."

"Call the sheriff, Damien. I mean it. Call him now. I'll confess everything if you'll promise to let me walk away."

"I can't do that. Besides, you could very well be right about Caudillo's connections. I don't see any other way he could remain under the law-enforcement radar."

"Which only makes my point more valid. Getting involved puts you in danger. This isn't your responsibility, Damien."

"That's where you and I have a difference of opinion, Emma. If I see a cow stuck in the mud, I don't stop to check the brand before I pull it out."

"But your neighbor doesn't shoot you."

"Good point. But I still have to do what I have to do. I don't plan to do anything stupid, Emma. I'm just getting a lay of the land."

"Fine. If there's no danger involved, you won't object to my going with you."

Damien shook his head. "You've been through enough, Emma. I can't let you torture yourself that way."

She knew he was right. Seeing the island would make her relive the misery and fear. But it wasn't as if she'd made giant strides in putting them behind her anyway.

"I can point things out as we fly over," she said, "like

the storage building where he keeps the crates of weapons. I saw that the night I escaped."

"You'll be better off here at the ranch with Belle," he insisted.

Belle. She'd almost forgotten she had a baby in her care. "I'll ask your mother if she can watch her."

Damien hooked his thumbs in his jeans pockets. "The sheriff said for you not to leave the area."

"Actually, he didn't. He put you in charge of knowing where I am at all times. And you gave him your word that you would. The only way you can guarantee that is if you take me with you."

Damien took her hands in his. "You're not going to let this go, are you?"

"No."

"Then let me go on record as saying I think this is a big mistake."

Her heart was still reeling from the feel of her hands inside his when he let go and backed away.

"I'll go make the needed arrangements with my brothers," he said. "You can talk to Mother, but I can pretty much guarantee that no matter what she had on her schedule for this afternoon and tomorrow, she'll cancel to stay home with Belle."

"What reason will I give her for going away overnight?"

"Tell her we're making a fast trip to visit your parents. She's big on family. She'll approve of that."

That would change fast if Carolina ever found out the truth about Emma's parents. But then there was no reason that she ever would.

Emma might be tremendously attracted to Damien, but they were not only from different worlds, they were from alternate universes. He'd gotten the silver spoon. She'd come closer to having a used Popsicle stick stuck in her mouth.

He had the perfect family. She had…

Nothing.

"On second thought, let's go with checking the references of a man who might be Belle's father," Damien said.

"That wouldn't require our staying all night."

"It could."

All night. Just the two of them. In a hotel in Miami.

Would Damien expect more than she could give? Or would she be the one disappointed when she climbed into bed alone? She had no idea what she was capable of feeling sexually or what would send her emotions tumbling down a black hole.

For that she hated Caudillo all the more.

"I DON'T KNOW HOW SHE'S done it, but this woman has definitely got you riding crooked in a slipping saddle."

"Her name is Emma," Damien said. "And to keep things straight, Durk, she doesn't have me doing anything. I'm making my own decisions."

"Hey, bros, we're on the same team here." Tague made the timeout signal. "Let's settle down and play it cool."

"I second that," Damien said. "I know my decisions may not be making a lot of sense to you right now, Durk, but you have to trust me on this."

"I'm trying, but it seems to me you're drilling the well before you have the geologist's report. What do you really know about Emma?"

"We had this discussion yesterday."

"Exactly. And now you're flying her down to Miami with you."

"There's a method to my seeming madness. It's not like I'm whirling her away on some wild romantic adventure."

"I wish the hell that was what this was about," Durk said. "I can understand romance, or even lust. It's all the clandestine undercurrents that go with Emma that worry me. Baby smuggling. A dead man. Cletus said—"

"Whoa. Stop there," Damien said, suddenly understanding the source of Durk's concerns. "I know what Cletus thinks, but he's an attorney. He's supposed to be suspicious of motive. I may be acting on instinct here, but that doesn't mean I'm not being cautious or smart."

"Then I guess I've said enough," Durk said, "but you know you're starting to act a lot like Dad. He always had a tendency to follow his instincts no matter what logic dictated."

"I was just thinking the same about you," Damien said, "but I was thinking in terms of his hardheaded tendencies."

"I'd say you're both acting like Dad," Tague said. "But I don't see that as a bad thing. Nine times out of ten, Dad came out on top of any venture he attempted."

"So it's a draw," Durk said. "As far as I know, both corporate jets are available tonight and tomorrow."

"They are," Damien said. "I checked this morning. I'll take the smaller one."

"What about a pilot?"

"I'll do the flying."

"I can go as backup," Tague said.

"I'd rather you stay here at the ranch and run interference in case the sheriff shows up. If he does, tell him we're in Dallas checking out a lead on the baby's father. Make it sound good. We're telling Mother the same. Keeps things less complicated."

"Lying to the law is serious," Durk reminded him.

"Believe me, if this eventually comes down the way I

hope it will, Sheriff Garcia will just be begging for a bit role in the movie."

"Then level with us soon," Durk said. He put a hand on Damien's shoulder. "And take no risks. You got that?"

"I've got it," Damien said. "Oh, and by the way, Tague— I need you to give that speech for me tomorrow night."

Tague grimaced. "Not only do I miss the excitement and the trip with a gorgeous woman, I get stuck at a podium giving your stuffy speech."

"Yep," Damien said, "but then who said life was fair?"

THEY LEFT THE RANCH AS soon as Carolina returned from teaching her Sunday School class. As Damien had suggested, she'd quickly volunteered to cancel her plans for the next two days for a chance to babysit Belle.

That put them in Dallas by noon. Fortunately for Emma, Damien had to make a quick stop at the offices of Lambert Inc. and had asked if she wanted to go with him or be dropped off at a nearby shopping center.

She jumped at the chance to shop. Emma was thankful for Carolina's clothes loans, but she was eager to pick up a few outfits of her own that actually fit. The first department that caught her eye was lingerie.

To her surprise, she was quickly seduced by a pair of lacy black panties and a matching bra that dipped low in front. And along with a pair of cute but sensible cotton pj's, she chose an eye-popping hot-pink chemise.

Maybe she was starting to come back to life on every level.

She visited two more stores in the mall, and an hour later she'd also purchased new makeup, two pairs of jeans, two shirts, two sweaters, a pair of tennis shoes and a cute pair of pewter ballerina-style flats—all on sale.

Her one splurge had been a flirty little black dress from

a selection of cruise clothing so that she wouldn't embarrass Damien at dinner tonight if they happened to go to some swanky restaurant.

He was waiting for her in the coffee shop where he'd told her he'd meet her, talking on his cell phone and nursing a cup of coffee. He broke the connection when he saw her and stood to greet her.

"Judging from the packages, I'd say you found everything you were looking for."

"Yes, did I take too long?"

"I was about to send out the search dogs," he said, reaching to relieve her of the packages.

"I'm sorry."

"And I'm kidding. That's the good thing about owning the plane. You don't have to worry about it leaving without you. And there's one more shop we should visit."

She followed his lead through the mall, practically running to keep up with his long stride. He stopped at the entrance to a store selling nothing but Western boots and hats.

"Look around," he said, "and see what you like."

"Boots are not in my budget. I have to make the money I have left last until I land a job. That could take a while since I have zero references." And going back to her old job was out of the question since that was the first place Caudillo would look for her.

"The boots and hat are my treat," Damien said.

She shook her head. "Accepting your help is one thing. Accepting expensive gifts is out of the question."

"Who said anything about expensive? Besides, you can't live on a ranch and not have boots and a Western hat."

"I don't live on a ranch. I'm visiting one."

"And everybody who visits the Bent Pine has to carry

their weight. That means brushing the horses, cleaning the stables, maybe even mending a fence or two. Boots are a basic necessity."

She picked up a pair and looked at the price printed on the bottom of the sole. "People actually pay that for boots?"

"Alligator," Damien said. "Nice for dress wear, but not very practical. Sit down and we'll have the salesman bring out a few pairs for you to try. You need the fit to be right in Western boots. Otherwise, your toes get squeezed."

"I don't know how or when I can pay you back."

"Sometimes a smile and a simple thank-you are all the payback a man wants or needs."

"I'll work at remembering that."

"Now, this is what I call an airplane."

Damien smiled and stood back for her to enter the cabin. "It does the job."

She hesitated for a second, as a terrifying thought popped into her head. Ten months ago she'd stepped onto a lavish yacht and into hell. At the time, she'd known Caudillo as long as she'd known Damien now.

Her legs grew weak and she started to shake.

Damien grabbed her arm to steady her. "Are you okay?"

This was Damien, not Caudillo. And he hadn't coaxed her onto the plane. She'd demanded that he let her go with him.

She knew his family. She'd left an innocent baby with his mother. She took a deep breath and regrouped. "Just a bit of déjà vu."

He muttered a curse. "You're thinking about the kidnapping." He tugged her around to face him and used his thumb to nudge her chin so that she was forced to meet his gaze. "Are you afraid of me, Emma?"

She read the incredulous look in the smoky depths of his eyes, and the truth hit so hard she felt dizzy. She wasn't only unafraid, she was falling hard for him. She could no longer convince herself it was a gratitude-based attraction. In spite of all she'd been through, or perhaps because of it, she'd let him into her heart.

"I'm not afraid of you, Damien. I just had a mini meltdown for a second there."

"Good, because if you're afraid of me, then I've done something terribly wrong to mislead you. But if you harbor a shadow of doubt about going on this trip with me, we can get off this plane right now and Tague can come and get you."

"No doubts." Except about her ability to cope with the tangled emotions that overrode her good sense.

"Tell me about the plane," she said, hoping to guide the conversation into safer territory.

"It's new. We—or rather Lambert Inc.—bought it after Dad's plane went down. Not that aircraft malfunction caused the crash that killed him, nor was he even in one of our planes. But his death emphasized the need for getting the safest small corporate jet on the market. The one we previously owned was getting on in years."

"Do you use it much in the ranching business?"

"More than you'd think. We do some innovative work at the ranch in feeding, breeding and even marketing, so I do quite a bit of guest lecturing at colleges with advanced animal-husbandry programs. And I like to see what ranchers in other parts of the country are doing, as well.

"We use it more frequently in the oil business, though. We own a larger jet, too, for moving personnel. Oddly, it comes out cheaper in the long run than constantly booking last-minute flights to drilling areas or chartering planes to handle hurricane preparedness when a storm kicks up in the Gulf."

"Are you involved in the oil part of Lambert Inc.?"

"I'm part owner, so I sit in on major decision making, though Durk's the CEO. He's always taken to that part of the business. Tague and I both love ranching. Dad left the business entirely to Mother, but she immediately split it four ways so that she, Tague, Durk and I all own equal shares."

"Ranching and oil. Isn't that an unusual mix?"

"Not in Texas. The ranch was in our family for generations, so when oil was discovered on the land, my grandfather expanded into drilling operations, as well."

"A good move," she acknowledged.

"The company's had its ups and downs, but then most do. Enough about business. All you have to do for the next few hours is sit back and relax. We'll stop and refuel near the halfway mark. The flight plan is already filed."

Emma dropped into a padded leather seat while Damien stored his small duffel and the stylish overnight bag Carolina had lent her.

She took a closer look at the plane's interior. There were oval windows and seating for six, and she could tell that four of the chairs reclined. It was much roomier and more comfortable than she'd expected of a plane this size.

"Toilet is in the front. There are refreshments in the back, though I'm not sure what. And there are usually some magazines in that small cabinet above the coffeepot."

"You sound as if you're planning to parachute out and leave me on my own."

"I'll be busy in the cockpit."

"Doing what?"

"Flying the plane. Though, to be honest, this baby practically flies herself."

"You're the pilot?"

"And you thought all I could do was ride horses and brand cattle."

"You constantly surprise me."

"And I'm just getting started. So sit back and buckle up. Weather's good all the way. You're in for one smooth ride."

And then a night in a Miami hotel with Damien. As screwed up as she was emotionally, how would she ever handle that?

So much for promises of a smooth ride.

HELL OF A DAY. EVEN ON Sunday, a man couldn't get any peace anymore, Sheriff Garcia lamented. No matter how many deputies the county hired, the worst of the mess always ended up on his desk. Taxpayers complained about his salary. He'd like to see them walk in his shoes for a day and sing that song.

He picked up the file Deputy Hagen had compiled for him on the stabbing victim out near Bent Pine Ranch and went straight to the fingerprint report.

Julio Gonzalez. Definitely in the system. Garcia scanned his mile-long rap sheet. Burglary, bad checks, using stolen credit cards, drunk and disorderly, sexual assault. He ran the gamut.

Fourteen arrests and… He counted in his head as he went through the lists. A total of six months and fourteen days in jail. Deported twice.

All the honorable, honest, hardworking, law-abiding Hispanics in the state of Texas, and Julio Gonzalez had to show up dead in his county and create a king-size head-ache and a ton of paperwork for Garcia.

But this gave all the credence he needed to Emma Smith's claim of self-defense. No cause to arrest her on murder charges, but he would need a bit more info from her to complete the bureaucratic reports. Mainly he needed her Social Security number.

If the baby weren't involved, he could have left it at that.

Garcia ran a quick check on the name Juan Perez in Dallas. There were no outstanding arrest warrants for anyone by that name. Always a good sign.

He shoved the paperwork to the back of his desk. Tomorrow would be soon enough to handle that.

He'd make the trip out to Bent Pine Ranch himself. It might give him a chance to see and talk to Carolina. Best catch in the state of Texas. Great looking for her age. Hell, she looked good for any age. More money than God. And she didn't have a mean bone in her body.

Not that she was anywhere near through grieving over Hugh. Not that he could fill Hugh Lambert's shoes. But then neither could anyone else in Texas.

It didn't hurt to remind Carolina that he was around and still aboveground for the day she did decide she needed a man.

DAMIEN ADJUSTED THE STRAP of Emma's travel bag, which he'd had to insist to the bellhop he was capable of carrying, and pushed the elevator button for the third floor. The hotel wasn't exactly what Damien had envisioned when he told the company travel agent intimate, comfortable and on the beach, but it would work. And it went a long way to helping him understand what she meant when she said "chic."

Emma had been exceptionally quiet on the taxi ride to South Beach and that worried him. He'd known a trip back to the Caribbean would upset her, but she hadn't given him a lot of choice in that.

If it was the two of them spending the night together

that concerned her, then welcome to the club. His feelings for her were all mixed-up with his need to protect her and a nagging suspicion that she still hadn't totally leveled with him.

That didn't make the physical attraction any less real, and it was growing stronger every second he was with her. They had some kind of inexplicable chemistry going on between them that the professors at Texas A&M had never covered in class.

But after what she'd been through with Caudillo, she needed a friend and protector a lot more than she needed some horny cowboy making a play for her just because his heart and head couldn't seem to keep things straight.

When they reached the room, he slid the key card and shoved open the door.

Emma let out an undecipherable cry and charged past him and into the room.

"Is something wrong?" he asked, following her to the double glass doors. "We can always change rooms or even hotels."

"Are you crazy? Look at that view. It's glorious."

He had to agree and he loved the joyous lilt in her voice. Maybe this was the perfect hotel after all.

She pushed the doors open and stepped outside. The wind caught her silky hair, tossing it around like summer hay. His chest tightened as the kind of lustful thoughts he shouldn't be having danced through his mind.

She turned to him. "May I use your phone? I want to call and check on Belle before I get too enthralled by the scenery."

"Sure thing." He handed it to her. "I'll use the hotel phone to have room service send up a bottle of wine. We can have it on the balcony. Red or white?"

"No. No wine." Desperation stole the lilt from her

voice. "I know this sounds weird, but it's just that Caudillo always…"

"'Nuff said," he interrupted.

"How about a beer instead," she offered. "I haven't had a cold beer in months."

"Now you're talking my language."

By the time he'd ordered the beers and a crabmeat appetizer, Emma was off the phone.

"All is well. Carolina said Belle is being a perfect baby," she announced as he joined her on the balcony.

"And I'm sure Mother is spoiling her rotten."

She handed him his phone. "Belle needs spoiling. She lost her mother."

The way Damien Briggs, the son of Melissa Briggs, had needed spoiling when he'd lost his mother. The nagging doubts that had plagued Damien when he first found the birth certificate set in again.

"Do you think a woman could ever love an adopted child the way she loves her biological one?" he asked.

"I think it depends on the mother. Some mothers don't even love their biological children. But if you're asking if I think it's possible, the answer is absolutely. Love doesn't shrink the heart. It grows it and makes room for more love."

"That sounds like something my mother would say."

"I didn't hear it from her, but I did hear it from a very wise lady. I hope to have lots of kids one day, both foster children and my own, and prove her right over and over again."

"They will be very lucky kids." Almost as lucky as the man who shared that family with her.

His mother would be the type who could love another woman's baby as deeply as she loved her own, especially if it were her sister's.

But not Hugh. Bloodline had been everything to him.

A knock at the door announced the arrival of room service.

"I'll get that," Damien said. His cell phone rang while he was signing the check. He took the call as he closed the door behind the waiter.

"Hope I didn't catch you at a bad time."

"No problem, Carson. What's up?"

"I just came upon a new tidbit of information concerning your man Caudillo that I thought might interest you."

"Keep talking."

"He's married to an American citizen who used to work for the ATF. They tied the knot on his yacht last year."

"Do you have the woman's name?"

"Emma Muran."

Chapter Nine

Damien's hand tightened on the phone. He'd been expecting some new twist to complicate things. He hadn't expected a complete shift in the dynamics. "How credible is the information?"

"A marriage license was filed in Aruba. The wedding itself took place on Caudillo's yacht while sailing on the Caribbean Sea. No exact location was given."

"Were you able to bring up a copy of the license?"

"Yes, but don't ask me specifics on how I did that."

"Wouldn't dream of it. Was the license officially signed and documented?"

"Signed by Anton Klein, Emma Louise Muran, the ship captain who conducted the ceremony and two witnesses."

"What's the date of the marriage?"

"March 13 of last year."

In the same month that Emma said she'd been kidnapped. Even the entanglements were becoming entangled.

"Don't know if that information is important in any way," Carson said, "but I thought I'd pass it on."

"You done good, pardner."

"I can't wait to hear what this quest to find out about Caudillo is about."

"One day soon." The sooner, the better.

"Take care and watch out for the bulls."

"The bulls are the least of my worries right now."

Damien thanked him again and dropped the phone into his pocket. Then he grabbed the beers and food and headed to the balcony. Unfortunately, the sunset daylight had faded to twilight.

So had his mood.

Durk just might be right. His faith in Emma might be triggered by a body part other than his brain. But he wasn't nearly ready to give up on her yet.

EMMA TOOK THE BEER FROM Damien's outstretched hand. "Weirdly, I still love the sound of the surf," she said as she settled back in the lounger. "At least Monster Man didn't steal that from me."

"Good."

She sipped her beer and tried one of the canapés. "These are good. What are they?"

"Crabmeat bites."

A tension that hadn't been there before settled between them. "Is something wrong?" she asked.

"It could be. Does the date March 13 mean anything to you?"

The crabmeat bite rolled in her stomach. She turned away from the beach and stared at Damien. "That was the day I was kidnapped."

"According to a document filed in Aruba, it was also the day you and Anton Klein—better known as Caudillo—were married."

She jerked up so that she was sitting ramrod straight on the edge of the lounger. The abrupt move tipped the beer bottle and sent cold liquid trickling down her arm. "You have got to be kidding."

"So you didn't marry him?"

"Not unless marriage in the Caribbean means drugging a woman and taking her prisoner."

"The wedding supposedly took place on his yacht."

"I was on his yacht that night, but he drugged me within minutes after I came on board, and when I woke up, we were speeding toward Enmascarado. And, believe me, I wasn't saying 'I do.'"

She stood and walked to the edge of the balcony and then it hit her. She spun around and glared at Damien, anger boiling inside her. "You actually considered the possibility that I might be married to Caudillo, didn't you?"

"It crossed my mind."

"So why are you really here tonight, Damien? If you still don't trust me, why are you sticking your neck on the chopping block? Is this some adrenaline rush for you, like skydiving or driving race cars?"

"No, I kinda like staying alive, and your getting indignant and all bent out of shape isn't going to help things."

"You think? I've told you things I thought I'd never speak of to anyone. I shared fears so real they haunt me day and night. And you think I forgot something like, 'Oh, yeah, it wasn't really a kidnapping. We got married'?" He walked over to the railing and reached for her hand. She pulled away.

"I believe you were held captive by Caudillo, Emma. I believe the stories of mental torture and that you're still running scared, afraid that he'll track you down and kill you. But look at this from my perspective."

"Which is?"

"You started presenting an elaborate array of lies from the second I met you. Fiction ebbed to truth in bits and pieces. How am I supposed to know when I have all the pieces?"

Her anger began to wane. There was really no reason

for him to trust her and every reason for him to have kicked her out of his house and out of his life the minute the sheriff showed up at his door.

"Point made," she said. "But just to be clear, there are no more crystals of truth to drop on you."

"Then we're good?"

"Yeah, Damien. We're good."

"Then how about another beer, because there are more new developments than just the nonexistent wedding."

"In that case I may need a full six-pack."

She stayed at the railing while he went for the beers, looking out at the silvery stream of moonlight dancing across the water while her mind tackled the news. Caudillo was evil to the core, but he was not a man to do things without a reason.

But how could faking a marriage to her help him? There was certainly no money to inherit. No prominent family name to benefit him. As far as she could see, he had nothing to gain by claiming her as a wife. And he'd definitely never planned on setting her free.

Damien rejoined her at the railing with two icy-cold beers.

"So what else have you learned about Caudillo?" she asked.

"This is more about you."

"About me? You're investigating me now?"

"I did a basic internet search on my computer over at ranch headquarters. I haven't put you at any risk."

"What am I supposed to have done now?"

"You were never reported as missing."

"You have to be wrong about that. Even from the islands, I was texting my friend Dorothy every day. And then I just dropped off the face of the earth. There's no way she wouldn't have reported me missing."

"Unless she got word you'd gotten married."

"No, especially not then. She'd know I wouldn't do something like that without talking to her about it. She'd have gone straight to the police when she couldn't get in touch with me, or at least within the first few days.

"And even if a catastrophe had befallen Dorothy, like a freak accident of some kind, I had a job that I never went back to. I had an apartment full of clothes. Surely someone would have gone to the cops and reported that I'd gone missing while vacationing in the Caribbean. The news media usually has a field day with something like that."

"And they didn't," Damien said. "I couldn't find one mention of your disappearance, not even in your hometown paper."

"I don't understand."

"For some reason, people must have thought you stayed away by choice."

"Well, I didn't, and I can't imagine why they'd think that, unless…"

She slapped her hands hard against the railing. "It's Caudillo. Somehow he's behind all of this. I don't know how, but I know he is. Let me use your phone again, Damien. I'm calling Dorothy right now."

Her fingers shook as she punched in the familiar number. The phone rang three times and then a woman answered.

"Is Dorothy there?"

"No, you must have the wrong number."

"Then this isn't Dorothy Paul's phone?"

"No. I've had this number since last March, but Dorothy must have had it before us. You're not the first person who's asked for her."

Emma felt the air leave her lungs as she thanked the

woman and broke the connection. She should be crying. Or screaming. Instead she felt numb.

"Dorothy's dead. Caudillo killed her, Damien. I know he did."

"Did the person on the phone tell you that?"

"No. She said I had the wrong number, but I didn't. The woman said she'd had that number since last March."

"Then you're jumping to conclusions."

"But knowing Caudillo as I do, it makes sense. Caudillo probably checked my phone and knew I'd texted her about meeting him. Then he killed her before she could say anything to the police."

"That's a big jump from a disconnected number, Emma."

"Not when you know Caudillo the way I do."

"Is there someone else you can call to find out about Dorothy?"

"I could contact someone at ATF."

"Let's hold off on that. I'll get someone on this first thing in the morning, but in the meantime, you need to try and keep a positive spin on this. Caudillo surely didn't kill everyone who knew you to keep them from reporting you missing. Something else is going on here. And there's no evidence that Dorothy is not alive and well with a new phone number."

"Dorothy did have a habit of changing her phone number when she dumped a boyfriend."

"I'll call my buddy and see if he can track down a number for Dorothy Paul in Nashville. So back to your disappearance going unreported. What about your parents or other members of your family? Have you contacted any of them since your escape?"

"I have no family."

"Care to elaborate on that?"

"Only once we've exhausted every other topic in the world. Next question."

"Whose idea was it to go to the Caribbean on your vacation?"

"Dorothy's. I wanted to go to Italy and then she convinced me we'd have more fun island-hopping. She'd hooked up with some beach bum she'd met in a chat room. The Skype affair died long before the trip."

"Did she say what happened?"

"No, she just stopped talking about him. That was typical of her chat-room boyfriends. They came and went as quickly as her real-live hookups. But don't get the wrong idea about her. She was smart and competitive and a super friend." Her voice broke again. She had to get a grip and hold on to it. Her emotions were so far out of sync, she'd need to get better to have a nervous breakdown.

"I think we've covered enough for now," Damien said. "How about dinner?"

"I've lost my appetite."

"Then come to the restaurant with me and keep me company while I have dinner."

"Do I have time to shower first?"

"All the time you want."

She gathered the empty bottles and leftovers and piled them just outside the hotel door for pickup. When she turned around, Damien was standing in a doorway that opened to an adjoining room.

"Which room do you want? They're a little different, but both have ocean views."

So the question of sleeping in his arms or scooting to the far edge of the bed in her cotton pajamas had never really been an option.

She wasn't sure she wanted to sleep in his arms. So why did it bother her that the decision had been made for her?

Because Damien didn't need her the way she needed him, that's why. His emotions were fine. He hadn't lived ten months with a madman.

She picked up her bag. "I'll take the other room."

And she'd keep the door shut. Not to keep him out, but to keep her in.

CAUDILLO WALKED INTO THE restaurant and was immediately swamped with attention. Ordinarily he loved the waitresses fawning over him like he was a rock star. Tonight, he really wanted to be left in peace to drink his wine alone. But it was important to keep up appearances, so he played the game.

"It is good to have you back. We haven't seen you in so long, Mr. Caudillo."

"Too long. I missed you and that delicious sweet fungi soup. I trust it's on the menu tonight."

"It's always on the menu. If not, I would have gone in the kitchen and made it for you myself."

The island beauty making the offer bent over so that he had a long, satisfying look at her perky breasts and the nipples that were barely covered by the bikini top of her uniform.

He'd see she was rewarded well tonight for her thoughtfulness. Unlike Emma, he didn't make her sick. But then Emma hadn't reacted to him that way at first. She'd played him. Slightly aloof. Coy. Classy. But the attraction had been more than evident in her eyes and in her smile.

Another of the beauties hurried out with a plate of tiny codfish cakes.

"Are the codfish fresh?" he asked.

"This morning they were swimming in the sea. And Alioto dipped them in her special mix of onions, peppers, flour and annatto oil, just the way you like them."

She moved in close as she set them on the table in front of him, swaying her hips so that her firm buttocks were even more pronounced. Yes, he'd been away from Misterioso much too long.

The young ladies continued their efforts to please him, knowing they'd reap ample compensation for their pampering. But even as they stimulated him, they didn't flush Emma from his mind.

They'd sat at this very table the night he'd met her. She'd thought it was by chance that they'd met that night, but Caudillo trusted little to chance.

He'd spotted her from the deck of his yacht even before it was anchored. He'd kept his binoculars directed at her for at least an hour.

He'd seen her fingers loosen the clasp of her bikini top when she was sunning. Had watched her rub the smooth, oily concoction on every inch of her exposed skin. Had been excited by the way the water shimmered on her flesh when she'd come out of the surf after a swim.

And even that hadn't been by chance. He'd come to the island that day just for her, and she hadn't disappointed—at least not then.

It wasn't her failure to provide him with ATF secrets that brought him the supreme regret. It was the humiliation and rejection. His touch had made her sick. Vomit from her stomach had slapped him in the face, even rolled into his nose and eyes and between his lips like a fetid kiss.

He could never bring himself to make love to her after that, could never trust her not to debase him with the revolting poison of her stomach's contents.

She should have been fed to the sharks then. But he couldn't bear to lose her. She haunted his mind when he was away from the island, and he couldn't wait to get back to her.

That was over now.

The plans were in place. Even if she were crazy enough to go to the FBI and accuse him of kidnapping her, no one would believe her. And if she lied about their marriage and accused him of kidnapping her, who'd believe her lies about his dealing in illegal arms?

He'd have to play it carefully for a while, but he could use a vacation anyway. Rio was nice this time of year. But first he had business in America.

He'd effectively neutralized Emma's threat to him. Having her killed would offer him no real satisfaction.

That's why he would take care of the job himself. He'd look her in the eyes while he tortured her the way he'd killed the others. He'd be standing next to her, perhaps even holding her hand when she begged for death.

And then he'd mercifully give her what she pleaded for.

THE CANDLELIT RESTAURANT where they'd had dinner had been romantically intimate with a breathtaking view of the breaking surf in the moonlight. The perfect setting for lovers. A painfully awkward setting for her and Damien.

The predinner conversation had set the tone for the evening. The disturbing new questions without answers created a medley of gloom and doom that couldn't be infiltrated by the setting or the food.

She'd picked at her meal of broiled fish, baked potato and salad. Damien had devoured his surf and turf. Now they were back at the hotel, and she had a trip to Enmascarado Island to look forward to in the morning.

"We could take a midnight stroll if you'd like," Damien offered as he closed the door behind them and turned the deadlock.

"Not tonight. I'm tired. I think I'll turn in."

"I'm thinking the same. I'd like to check out of the hotel

by seven in the morning, if that's okay with you. We'll grab some breakfast on the way to the airport."

"How can you possibly think of food after all you just ate?"

"Cowboys have a rough life. We need nourishment."

"You do see yourself as a cowboy, don't you?"

His eyebrows arched. "What do you see me as? Or dare I ask?"

"I don't know you well enough to answer that question."

"That's not true," Damien said. "You haven't known me long, but you know me well. We've had more deep conversations than I've had with some women I dated for months."

"Okay." She might as well be honest. "I see you as a wealthy rancher who jets around the country at the spur of a moment. A man used to being in charge who makes a few phone calls and has everyone jumping to do his bidding. A successful entrepreneur who walks into a mall and buys what he fancies without looking at prices."

"Wow. If that's all you see in me, I can't believe you're here."

"I wasn't finished."

"Can we jump ahead to some of the good stuff—if there is any good stuff?"

"None of that is bad, Damien. It's how it is. I also see you as a man with scruples and values and the determination to do what's right no matter the risk. I see you as a man who loves his family, his home, his land and his livestock. I see you as a man who keeps his promises. A man who protects people who need protecting."

"And now you've just described what it is to be a cowboy. Well, except you left out that we're smart enough to know not to squat with our spurs on."

"I also failed to mention that you always know how to defuse a situation and make me smile."

He stepped closer and trailed a finger down her cheek and all the way to her collarbone. "Did I mention how great you look in that dress?"

"Not more than a half-dozen times."

His cell phone rang. He ignored it.

"Aren't you going to answer your phone?" she asked.

"So that's why I'm hearing bells. If we wait a minute it will stop ringing."

"You can't do that. It might be your mother. It might be something to do with Belle."

He put his hands up in surrender and then checked the ID. "It's Tague. I'd better take it."

"You should. And we both should get some sleep. Good night, Damien."

She hurried away before he could protest and before something got started that would backfire on them. She went to the adjoining room, opened the curtains and stared out the glass doors at the star-studded sky.

In March she'd gone to paradise and found hell. Now she'd gone to Texas and found Damien. The first had ruined her life and left her an emotional wreck. The second was likely going to break her heart.

She was not what the cowboy needed, and he'd realize that as soon as he was through saving her.

She unzipped her travel case and pulled out the Nordstrom bag she'd tucked inside it while they were still on the plane. She retrieved the pajamas and tossed them onto the bed.

Unable to help herself, she reached back inside and tangled her fingers in the silky chemise. She picked it up and held the sexy nightie in front of her as she approached the full-length mirror on her closet door.

She hardly recognized the woman staring back at her. No wonder the chemise had tempted her. It was nothing like the slutty evening wear that Caudillo had made her wear for him.

Instead she saw the Emma she used to be. A woman not afraid of looking smokin' hot on occasion. A woman who'd been bucking for a promotion with the ATF. A woman who'd gone on vacation alone rather than lose the money she'd already invested.

A woman who'd stupidly boarded a luxurious yacht with a mysterious stranger.

Unexpected tears pooled in her eyes. Now she was a woman afraid to live, because if she did, Caudillo would find her again.

Damien knocked once on the door she'd left ajar. "How about a nightcap to help you sleep?"

She looked up and saw Damien's face reflected in the mirror, though he was still standing near the door.

She dropped the chemise and it pooled on the floor, leaving her feeling incredibly exposed even though she was still wearing the black dress.

A second later Damien's arms wrapped around her from behind.

She turned, and with tears she could neither explain nor stop streaming down her face, she lifted her mouth to his and melted in his kiss.

Chapter Ten

Damien only meant to hold Emma, but the second their lips touched, the pent-up frustration and desire erupted inside him. He'd ached to kiss her practically since the moment they'd met.

The thrill of her touch ripped through him, making him rock hard, the passion so hot it felt as if it were singeing his brain. When he came up for air, he kissed her eyelids, the tip of her nose, her earlobe, the soft, sensual column of her neck.

His hands splayed her back, pulling her closer. When she moaned, he lifted her from the floor and held his breath as he let her ride down the length of his erection. His hands found the zipper of her dress and tugged it low enough that her breasts spilled out of the bodice.

"Oh, Emma…"

And then somehow a tiny measure of sense reached his crazed brain. He pulled away, though the need inside him was still ravaging his body.

"What's wrong?" she asked.

"Me, coming at you like an animal."

"Is that what that was, just animal magnetism?"

The hurt in her voice was like a fist to the gut. "It's not all it was, not even close. But I had no right, not after what you've been through, not when your emotions are still all over the place. You're just too damn vulnerable."

"You're right, Damien. You're always right, and that's starting to annoy me. I am trying to move on. I escaped the monster, but he's in my head, and the horrors pop up when I least need them to be there."

"I know. But you'll get there, Emma. You're the most determined woman I've ever met. And you definitely have the most spunk."

"For the record, I wasn't thinking about Caudillo when we were kissing. I wasn't thinking at all."

"And I want to kiss you again, Emma. I want to make love with you so bad it's killing me. But when we make love, I want to be certain you have no regrets. I want you to be as ready for that step as I am."

"I've never had anyone *not* make love to me so sweetly, Damien."

"I'll tell myself that all the way through the cold shower I'm about to take. But do me a favor, Emma."

"Anything."

"Keep that hot-pink negligee with you at all times, so when the time is right, that's what you'll be wearing when we start."

"That, Damien Lambert, is a promise I will gladly keep."

He turned and left quickly, not daring to kiss her goodnight. He left the door between them ajar just in case she had a nightmare and needed him during the night.

Tonight he could come to her rescue. Tomorrow morning, he'd be flying her back to the war zone.

He wasn't at all sure that was in the cowboy code.

EMMA WAS IN THE COCKPIT with Damien when Enmascarado first came into view. She braced herself for an attack of nerves or paralyzing dread and prepared to run in case she got sick. The last thing they needed was for her to throw up all over the controls.

Amazingly, her hands didn't sweat, her stomach didn't roll and her chest didn't cave in. Either her nerves were actually making progress or else being in Damien's presence made her feel safe.

The vantage point helped, too, and the fact that the yacht was nowhere to be seen, which meant that Caudillo wasn't there, either. The fortress was less intimidating than she remembered, the island much smaller. At least it was until Damien began dropping altitude.

"I'll be working the controls so that we can circle the island. You do the talking—anytime you're ready to start. We'd be able to see all of the island at once were it not for the trees and heavy vegetation. This whole island is barely twice the size of the Bent Pine Ranch."

"Bear in mind that I only saw a small part of it," she reminded him. "I arrived at night. And once I was here, I was confined within the walls surrounding the house."

"Just tell me what you know. The north side of the island is just below us."

"That's the house," Emma said. "The small inlet about a hundred yards down the beach from the house is where he anchors the yacht."

"That looks more like a commercial marina than a personal boat dock."

"It is, except that Caudillo is the only customer allowed. There were at least two dozen workers there the night we arrived. I was still woozy, but I remember that they helped us off the boat and, I suppose, cleaned it and got it ready for the next trip. Before I was drugged I remember noting that the yacht was immaculate, more like a posh hotel than a boat."

"Tell me about the house."

"Only if you promise you're not going there to try to deal with Caudillo yourself."

"We've already established that, but you have to admit it would be fun to see the look on his face if you dropped in with a team of Navy SEALs and told him that you were back for your half of the property settlement."

"Don't even joke about my going back to the island or about a marriage."

"Right. No jokes. But you did crack a smile. I'll circle the north end again in a minute, but what are the buildings to the west?"

"I have no idea. I didn't know they were there."

"Could be barracks for his army. Did you ever hear him say how many men worked for him?"

"No, but when he was gone I could hear them outside the house. My guess is there had to be at least fifty in all, counting the guards at the house. There could be more."

"So it appears no one around here questions a businessman's need for an army," Damien said.

"I don't think anyone questions Caudillo about anything."

"Then I suspect he pays off the right people. Corruption is always in style."

"It is his personal island," Emma reminded him. "He told me it was a gift from some prince I'd never heard of, but he could have been lying."

"I guess real estate is real estate," Damien said, "as long as you have the money to pay someone off." He pointed to his left. "There, just over the guava trees, do you have any idea what that rectangular building is used for?"

"That, I do know. It's where the men were hauling the crates of weapons from the night I escaped. On the beach just past that is the dock where their boat was."

"And then there's another view of the house coming in from the south. I can see why you think it looks like a fortress with that stone fence all the way around it. Nothing is missing but a moat."

"No moat. You walk through the front doors and into the main part of the house. It's a big open room with no furniture. I never saw it used for anything other than a giant foyer."

"Where were you kept?"

"My quarters were to the right."

"What about the other two women who were there for part of the time you were? Where were their quarters?"

"I'm not sure, but not close enough that I could communicate with them through the walls."

"So there could be other women still imprisoned there who you never saw."

"It's possible." Suddenly, the light came on. She should have realized it before. The questions. The flyover. The entire trip to the Caribbean.

Damien might not be planning to personally lead his own rescue operation, but he was planning to make sure one was carried out utilizing whatever information he culled from the trip.

"You're going to the FBI with this information, aren't you, Damien?"

"Let's not get into that now."

"And if Caudillo has connections with the FBI as he said, how long do you think it will take him to find me?"

"He's never going to find you because I won't do anything unless I'm positive you're safe. And face it, Emma, you are never going to feel safe until Caudillo's either dead or behind bars. And for all we know, Caudillo might already be picking out your replacement. This man has to be stopped."

She took a deep breath and fought back the wall of fear that held her captive as surely as Caudillo had. She'd stopped lying to Damien. It was time she stopped lying to herself.

"I agree that Caudillo has to be stopped at any cost, Damien. In my heart, I've always known that I couldn't just run away and soothe my conscience with some anonymous phone call. But the thought of facing him again is frightening beyond anything I can describe."

"You have every right to be afraid, but I'm not going to lose you to that fear, Emma." He took her hand and squeezed it. "I don't plan to lose you at all."

"THAT'S THE ISLAND OF Misterioso just below us now," Damien said.

Emma leaned to her right for a better view. "It looks like a kite from here."

"Shall I lower the altitude to see if you can pinpoint the hotel you fell in love with?"

"I think it's at the end of the kite's tail. But no. I don't need to see it. I'm out of love with it now. It's where I met the monster."

"The beaches look great," Damien said, "but they don't have a decent landing strip on the island, so you have to get there by boat or helicopter or in a very small plane."

"That's why we'd already arranged for a charter boat before I got to Aruba," Emma said. "Actually, I could have gotten a much better rate if I'd booked on-site, but Dorothy had her heart set on going to one of the non-touristy islands."

"Dorothy had a lot of plans for a woman who canceled out at the last minute."

"I told you. It was a money issue. And I was fully in favor of going to Misterioso."

"How did you hear about it? Did you go through a travel agent?"

"No. Dorothy looked it all up on the internet."

"And then she decided to bail on you."

"I'm not blaming her. She was heartsick over missing the trip, and she couldn't possibly have foreseen what would happen to me if I came alone. And if I hadn't come alone, we might have both been kidnapped. I know she would have jumped at the chance to board that fabulous yacht."

Still, the facts didn't add up for Damien. It was Dorothy's dream vacation and her friend went without her. Yet Dorothy hadn't bothered to report it to authorities when Emma had stopped texting and had never come home.

He wouldn't bring that up now. He'd heard the sadness in Emma's voice when she talked about her friend. She thought Dorothy might be dead. He had other ideas about that, but he didn't want to say anything more to upset Emma.

He circled the island again at a lower altitude so that he could get a better look at the three yachts he'd noticed anchored in a small inlet.

Emma turned and touched his sleeve. "That's it, Damien. The biggest one. That's Caudillo's yacht."

"Are you sure?"

"I'm sure. How many yachts that size can there be in the world, much less in the Caribbean?"

"Not too many."

"If the yacht is there, Caudillo is not far away. If we had one of those sophisticated drones the army uses, we could fire it on him and blow him to smithereens."

Her voice was clipped as if she were firing off shells. Killer thoughts claimed Damien's mind, as well. He'd like to walk onto that yacht and strangle the sick bastard with his bare hands.

Possibilities stormed his mind. He tried to put them in some kind of rational order. He could land on one of the other islands and hire a boat to bring him and Emma back to Misterioso. They could go to whoever was in charge on this island and press charges.

The authorities surely couldn't just let Caudillo sail away if she was standing there telling them how he'd kept her captive. At least not in a perfect world. In this one, Caudillo was a regular on the island. He and Emma were outsiders. There was no question whose side they'd take.

Damien could call the FBI and request urgent help, but when they checked the records, they'd find that Emma Muran was married to Caudillo. The kidnapping story would instantly lose much of its credibility and urgency, especially since she wasn't being held captive now.

That explained the marriage license. It was Caudillo's insurance against kidnapping charges. For all Damien knew, the fake paperwork might have been filed in the past few days, after Emma's escape.

As he pondered the options, the yacht began to move. Damien circled again and increased his altitude. Then he watched helplessly as the yacht sailed not toward Enmascarado but toward the open sea.

"I hope he gets caught in one of those killer waves you read about and the ship sinks with him on it," Emma said.

"Good plan."

But in case that didn't happen, Damien figured he better come up with a plan of his own, one that had a lot better chance of succeeding. A plan where the FBI eagerly jumped into the fight with him.

For that, he might need a live Dorothy Paul.

And the time was ripe to renegotiate his earlier promise with Emma. The Lambert brothers did their best work as a team.

"HOME AGAIN," DAMIEN SAID as he stopped in the carport attached to the four-car garage on the Bent Pine Ranch. "Take a deep breath and let the odors of manure and damp earth titillate your lungs."

"I hope you're not planning to stop raising cattle and take up writing poetry."

"Always a critic in the group."

"But I'm as excited to be back to the ranch as you are. I can't wait to see Belle."

"Head on in and snatch her from Mother's clutches. I'll bring the luggage."

"Your mother will ask about what we found out about Belle's father."

"Tell her the lead didn't pan out."

"I hate lying to her."

"You can choose to tell her the truth anytime."

"I'd only drag her into the Caudillo sphere of horror. What I really need to do is leave Belle in her care and disappear the way I'd originally planned. You have plenty of information now to take this to the FBI, CIA, Homeland Security or the ATF."

"Here we go again. Run, baby, run."

"It's the only sensible solution."

"It's *no* solution. And I'm not ready to turn this over to any federal agency just yet."

"What's holding you back?"

"The kidnapping is compromised by the fake marriage license, and if Caudillo does have the connections he claims, a search of his island for illegal weapons would likely result in a dry run. He could clear the contraband off the island as quickly as the marauders did the night you escaped."

"I hadn't thought about that."

"If we go to the FBI with what we have now, the case against Caudillo could get so tangled in bureaucratic red tape it'll end up in file thirteen."

"And you don't have anything else. Face it, Damien. We've hit a brick wall. Caudillo wins."

"Not unless we give up, and I have no intention of doing that. Now, go see Belle."

She practically ran up the steps and across the wide porch. He'd always liked coming home to Bent Pine. But never had it looked or felt as good as it did now with Emma on the scene.

His phone rang as he slid the luggage straps over his shoulder. As always, he checked his caller ID. It was the private investigator he'd hired to find Belle's father.

"What's up?" he asked in lieu of hello.

"I may have good news for you."

"Hit me with it."

"I think I've located the Juan Perez you're searching for."

Chapter Eleven

"Tell me about the man you've located," Damien said.

"To start with, he's the only decent lead I've found. The downside is he lives in Fort Worth, not Dallas."

"Not a big deal," Damien admitted. People from outside the region frequently referred to the entire metropolitan area as Dallas or Dallas/Fort Worth, whether it was Fort Worth, Garland, Arlington or any number of smaller towns that surrounded Dallas.

Damien thought of himself as living in Dallas, though he was a good forty-five minutes from the downtown area, and that was when traffic was light.

"This Perez is in construction," the P.I. reported, "and has been with the same company for six years. No police record. No one is suing him for bad debts. And according to his landlord, he pays his rent on time."

"All to his credit, but I fail to see the connection between any of that and his being Belle's parent—other than his name."

"I'm coming to the evidential facts. He's twenty-nine years old and not married. He was born in Texas, so there's no question of his being legal. His neighbor says he's heard him say he sends money to his family and a pregnant girlfriend back in Mexico. But he says the guy hadn't mentioned that lately, so I figured she could have delivered the infant you're talking about by now."

"Have you met this Perez?"

"Not yet, but I drove by the construction site where he was installing windows. I picked him out from a picture I got off his website."

"He has a website?"

"Yeah. He refurbishes golf carts as a sideline business."

"When do you find out if he has a daughter named Belle?"

"Hopefully this evening. He stops off for a beer most nights after work. I'll be at his usual hangout tonight. A little small talk should let me know if we need to question him further."

"Tell you what. Email me the link for his website and the name and location of the bar he frequents and leave the rest to me."

"Then you don't want me to finish this investigation?"

"I don't want you to confront this man. If he turns out not to be the Juan Perez I'm looking for, I'll turn the case back over to you."

"Okay. Keep me posted."

"Will do, but get that information to me in the next few minutes."

Damien had mixed emotions about finding Belle's father. He knew returning the child to her biological father was the right thing to do. But once Belle was out of Emma's life, keeping Emma from leaving the Bent Pine would become increasingly difficult.

Keeping her with him was the only way he could keep her safe. He had to move fast on the Caudillo case—for all their sakes.

His phone rang again.

This time the news was all bad.

CAROLINA SAT IN THE MIDDLE of the family room floor surrounded by her treasures. She'd carefully removed each sentimental memento from one of the boxes she'd stored in the attic years ago.

Straightening her full skirt, she reached for the red heart-shaped box. Cradling it in her hands as lovingly as she'd cradled Belle in her arms, she caressed the brocade covering.

Hugh had given her that box and the sapphire ring inside it on their first anniversary. Their real anniversary, not the one he'd adopted so that Damien would never know he was born before they were married.

The band was engraved with the words Yours Forever. She still had the ring. She no longer had Hugh. Her dreams of growing old with him had gone down with the plane.

She looked up as Emma stepped into the room with Belle against her chest, her head resting on Emma's shoulder.

"I'm sorry," Emma said. "I didn't realize you were in here."

"That's okay. Come join me. I'm just delving into memories, and I've already been at it too long. I can use some company."

"If you're sure."

"I'm sure, if you don't mind talking to a sentimental old widow. Sybil and Pearl both avoid me when I get in these moods. So do my sons."

Emma sat down on the floor amidst the souvenirs. Carolina picked up a snapshot that had brought tears to her eyes a few minutes before. This time she smiled. That's the way it went with memories.

"This is Hugh the first time he tried to give Damien a bath by himself. They were both soaked, and so was my floor."

Emma reached for the picture for a closer look. "How old was Damien when this was taken?"

"Six months. I don't think Hugh got up the courage to bathe him again until he was walking. To tell you the truth, I was almost as inept with Damien as Hugh was. Neither of us had ever been around babies. Poor Damien. He was our guinea pig on parenting."

"You obviously did a lot of things right."

"He did turn out to be quite the man. Both Hugh and I were proud of all our sons."

"You must still miss your husband very much."

"Every waking minute."

"What was he like?"

"I could take hours answering that question. But I won't," she added quickly, lest she scare Emma off. "I guess the best description of Hugh is that he was bigger than life. He walked into a room and everyone else faded into the background. He was gregarious, boisterous and a man of his word."

"The two of you created a great life."

"Huge loved this ranch. He liked the business world, too, but the land was like an extension of him."

"He must have been a remarkable man."

"He was, but admittedly not quite as perfect as I make him sound. He had a tendency to believe that he always knew best. Damien inherited that trait from him. I suppose you've realized that by now."

Emma smiled. "He does like to be the boss."

"So you can imagine how often he and Hugh butted heads."

"How did you meet Hugh?"

"Ah, now, that's an afternoon in itself, but I'll give you the short-and-sweet version. I was working in the office of a team of neurosurgeons. One day this gorgeous man walked up to the desk, and when he smiled at me, I practically swooned. Unfortunately, Hugh was there with his father, who had a very aggressive brain cancer."

"Were they able to save him?"

"No, he died two months later. Hugh was living in a penthouse condominium in Dallas and was CEO of Lambert Inc. at the time. When his father died, he decided to name a new CEO and move back to the ranch. The night he told me of his plans was the same night he proposed. It took less than a heartbeat for me to say yes."

"That was pretty chancy, marrying a man you'd only known two months."

"It was quite a chance. Quiet, working girl marrying an affluent and vociferous oilman."

"Not your typical soul mates," Emma said.

"Far from it, but we were crazy in love. Little did I know then that I was in for the ride of my life."

"And you never had any regrets?"

"Only that it ended too soon." She brushed away a tear with the back of her hand. "When it comes time to marry, choose love over everything else, Emma. Always choose love."

Carolina stretched and massaged a kink in her neck. "Now I should get up from here and clean up this mess. And I don't know how I forgot to mention this, but the sheriff stopped by to see you this morning."

"What did he want?"

"To tell you that he was officially ruling Julio's death as self-defense."

"Great. That makes my day."

"He's going to call you later. He said something about needing your Social Security number to complete his paperwork."

Emma had said that the news made her day, and indeed

it should have at least brought a smile to her face. But Carolina couldn't help but notice the worry lines that were etched into her face.

The same way they'd been etched into Damien's face when he and Emma had returned a couple of hours ago. Her mother's instinct told her the strain had to do with more than just locating Belle's father.

"If you ever need anything, Emma, don't hesitate to ask. Or if you want to talk I'm available for that, too."

"Actually, I need to make a few long-distance phone calls. Would you mind if I use your phone? I'll pay you for the calls."

"Call anyone you want. We get unlimited long-distance."

"Thanks. Now if you'll excuse me, I'll go make the calls before Belle decides it's time to eat again."

Carolina picked up the picture of Damien and Hugh again.

I really wish you were here now, Hugh. Something is troubling Emma and Damien, and I think he could desperately use your advice.

If you're looking down on him, give him a hand. But leave off the lecture this time.

EMMA STRUGGLED TO FIGHT OFF yet another panic attack. You'd think fate would grant her a break every now and then.

Carolina had made it sound so incidental. The sheriff wanted her Social Security number.

If Emma gave him her real number, he'd find out she'd lied about her name being Emma Smith. If she gave him a fake number, he'd still find out she'd lied.

Either way, lying to him would undoubtedly lead to his reopening the investigation. It was a lose-lose situation.

And all for nothing. Telling him her real name would have been fine. No one had been looking for her when she'd been kidnapped. No one had ever looked for her.

All the nights she'd comforted herself with the belief that people were searching everywhere for her... All the times she'd convinced herself that someone would surely tie her disappearance from Misterioso Island to Caudillo and come to her rescue... It had been a sad, sick joke.

After the terrifying months she'd spent imprisoned on that horrible island, she was now about to be arrested and locked up again. The irony didn't stop there. This time she had been accused of murdering an animal who'd tried to rape her.

Damien was certain he could fix everything. But he couldn't.

In the end, Caudillo would win. He'd kill her and then sail away to exotic ports in his lavish yacht and laugh at their efforts to bring him down.

She looked up at a tap on her door. "Come in."

Damien stepped inside. "I have good news."

The look on his face suggested it wasn't. "What is it?"

"The detective thinks he may have located Belle's father. I'm going into Fort Worth to check out the lead."

"When are you going?"

He glanced at his watch. "In about ten minutes."

Emma took a step backward as a bizarre sinking sensation overtook her, as if she were being pulled into a dangerous current. She struggled to get hold of her emotions. She should be hopeful this would work out. Belle needed her father. And once she was with him, Emma was free to leave the Bent Pine.

She'd lose both Belle and Damien, but eventually she'd lose them both anyway. She had no claim on either of them. And even if she did, Caudillo would find her too easily here.

"I'm going with you, Damien. And no arguing this time. If I'm going to release Belle into this man's care, I have to know he's the real father and that he'll take good care of her."

"Then meet me at the truck in ten minutes."

She'd be there in five. At least this way she was doing something.

THE BAR WAS CROWDED AND NOISY.

"There's a small table in the corner," she said, nodding in that direction.

"I have a better view from here," Damien said as he scanned the room. "I'd like to size him up before we approach him."

Emma scanned the room as well but saw no one who resembled the computer printout photo Damien had shown her on the drive into Fort Worth.

"He's standing at the far end of the bar," Damien said. "Wearing the blue plaid sport shirt and a pair of what looks to be new jeans. Apparently, he changed out of his work clothes between here and the construction site."

With that description, Emma spotted Juan Perez quickly. He lifted a can of beer and chugged it down. Then he leaned over a young woman standing next to him and grinned as if she'd just said something tantalizingly entertaining.

Anger fired inside Emma. "If's that's Belle's father, he doesn't deserve her. Not when the ill mother of his child died trying to get his baby to him."

"Don't jump to conclusions."

"I already have. I don't like him—not that my opinion changes anything. How do we do this? I mean, we can't just step up to the bar beside him and tell him his Mexican girlfriend is dead and his kid is in the States."

A waitress stopped at Damien's elbow and smiled at him as if he were the knight in denim armor she'd been waiting for all her life.

"What can I get you?"

He turned to Emma. "How about a margarita?"

"Nothing for me," she said. "Not yet."

"I'll have a Lone Star."

"Want to run a tab?"

"Sure. We may be here for a while—but we're moving to the empty table in the back."

"No problem. I'll find you wherever."

"I'll just bet she would," Emma said when the waitress walked away.

"It's all about the tips."

Emma was almost certain that Damien had no idea the effect he had on women. It was more than his rugged good looks. It was his stance, his swagger, the vibe he put off. He was a man in control but without being controlling. Few men pulled it off so well. None that she'd ever met.

She took one of the chairs at the new table and watched as Damien approached Juan. She couldn't hear the conversation, but she saw Damien motion to the bartender to bring the man another beer. When he got his beer, the two of them joined Emma at the table.

"So exactly how is it you know my parents?" Juan asked.

"Actually, it's the mother of your daughter we know," Damien said.

Juan scooted his chair back a few inches and put up his hand as if warding off blows. "You've got the wrong man. I don't have a daughter."

"Did you have a pregnant girlfriend in Mexico?"

"I thought so, but turned out it wasn't my kid."

"How do you know that?" Emma asked.

"She told me when she decided to marry the other guy. So now I don't even have a girlfriend. I was working on changing that when you interrupted."

"When was the last time you talked to the girlfriend in Mexico?" Damien asked.

"A few months back when she called to blow me off. But my mother told me she had the baby just last week. It's a boy." Juan pushed back from the table and stood. "Look, I don't know how you got my name, but you have the wrong guy."

"And you're sure you don't have a two-month-old daughter named Belle?"

"You got it. I hope you find whoever it is you're looking for, but believe me, it ain't me."

Relief washed over Emma, but she didn't want to examine it too closely. She might find that she was relieved that she didn't have to give up Belle yet, instead of being glad she didn't have to give her up to a man she didn't like.

"It looks as if we made the trip to Fort Worth for nothing," Emma said.

"But since we're here, I know a great little Italian restaurant where we can have dinner."

"We should check with your mother first. She may have plans for the evening."

"I checked before we left home," Damien said. "She said to stay as late as we wanted. She seemed to be in a really down mood, so if anything, watching Belle may help her out of the dumps."

"She misses your father very much."

"I know. She keeps reminding all of us that healing from grief is not instantaneous. She says it ebbs and flows."

"Then we should definitely give her this time with Belle. Besides, I have a serious problem I should probably discuss with you."

"If it's that serious, we should have that margarita first."

"Bring it on."

A drink in a neighborhood bar where music blared from a jukebox and chatter and laughter filled the room. It seemed so natural, as if this were real and the hellish life on Enmascarado Island had been only a nightmare.

To trust that fallacy would be a deadly mistake. But right now all she could think of was the man who was sitting next to her and melting her resolve.

She had to snap out of this, and the best way to do that was to jump right back into the complicated web of lies and danger.

Once she'd tasted a few sips of the margarita, she took a deep breath and plunged into the next dilemma.

"I fully expect Sheriff Garcia to haul me away in cuffs within the next couple of days."

Damien shook his head. "Not a chance. He's already ruled Julio's murder self-defense. Mother said she'd told you that."

"Yes, but now he wants my Social Security number. When he finds out I lied about my name, he's almost certain to arrest me."

"Just give him your real number and your real name. Tell him you lied because you panicked. He won't press charges."

"How can you be so sure?"

"He knows Carolina likes you. He's not going to mess with the friend of someone who makes sizable contributions to his campaign."

"So he ruled Julio's death self-defense strictly based on

the fact that I'm staying at the Bent Pine? That sounds a lot like corruption."

"It was self-defense, Emma. Let's just go with the theory that the sheriff was smart enough to recognize that."

"So you think it's a nonissue?"

"I'm sure of it."

She finished her margarita in record time. It was the first one she'd had since the kidnapping, and in spite of everything, being here with Damien made it taste even better than she remembered.

They lingered with their drinks, not talking, but oddly comfortable with just being together. Emma struggled to stay in the present for a few minutes and to block Caudillo from her thoughts. She needed this moment to hold on to when Damien was just an old memory.

If she lived that long.

A country ballad started to play and the dance floor suddenly became crowded. Emma tapped her toe to the beat.

Damien laid his hand on top of hers. "Would you like to dance?"

"Yes. I'd like that." They got up and he took her hand and led her to the dance floor.

He held her close, their bodies touching as they swayed to the music. When the music stopped, he didn't move away. She looked up and met his gaze. The desire she saw in his eyes was hypnotic.

His lips lowered and touched hers. She melted into the kiss, her pulse exploding like fireworks.

But then a shudder started deep inside her and she felt as if Caudillo's shadow had fallen over her, making everything dark. She stiffened and pulled away.

"I'm sorry if I came on too fast."

"It wasn't you." She fought back tears.

"It's okay, Emma. You need time. I understand."

"I guess maybe horror ebbs and flows like grief," she said. "Recovery is definitely not instantaneous."

"He's not behind you yet, Emma. When he is, your real recovery can start. And he and his threats will be out of the picture one day soon. I promise you that."

But Damien couldn't know what he was up against.

Damien led her from the dance floor as a new crowd of dancers gathered around them. "How about dinner now?"

But she wasn't sure her emotions could handle an intimate dinner with Damien. "If you don't mind, I'd rather just grab a burger and head back to the ranch."

"Then a burger it is."

"If you don't stop being so accommodating, you may never get rid of me."

"Who said I want to?"

DAMIEN DID NOT SHOW UP FOR breakfast the next morning. Nor had he shown up by midmorning when Emma and Belle joined Carolina on the back porch.

Belle was having an exceptionally good day. Emma had spread a blanket on the sofa next to her and then placed Belle on it so that she could kick and swing her short arms at will while Emma kept careful watch.

"You're just being a real sweetheart this morning, aren't you, Belle? I think you like it here. Did you have fun without me last night?"

"I'm not sure how much she liked it," Carolina said, "but she kept us entertained. Grandma talked to her more than she's talked to Sybil in the last month."

"You certainly get along well with your in-laws," Emma said. "Have they always lived here with you and your family?"

"Pearl has," Carolina said. "Only, she didn't live with

us as much as we moved in with her. Remember I told you that Hugh had a penthouse condo in Dallas up until his father died from the brain tumor? He moved here then and when we married, Pearl turned over the master suite to us."

"What a thoughtful thing to do."

"Yes, except that I felt as if I'd displaced her. She ignored my protests, said she couldn't bring herself to sleep in the bedroom that she'd shared with her husband all those years. I didn't understand that then, but I'm beginning to."

"Maybe you'll feel differently in time."

"Perhaps, but this house is meant for raising families. It will belong to Damien when I die, so I'd be just as happy to turn the main wing over to him when he's ready to marry and begin a family of his own."

"What about Tague and Durk?"

"They'll each own one-third of everything when I'm gone except the house. Hugh insisted that as firstborn Damien be the one to keep the house that has been in the family for generations. But I fully expect Tague and Durk to build their own houses on the ranch when they marry, even though Durk will likely always have a place in town. Their roots to the ranch run deep."

"I'm sure they must."

"And you asked about Sybil. She came to live with me ten years ago when her husband died. He was a general in the army, but even though he was from the D.C. area and had traveled all his life, he loved it here on the ranch. They'd planned to retire here, but he had a heart attack one year before he could make that move. Naturally, I invited Sybil to move in with us. There's plenty of room here for everyone to have their own space."

"I find it remarkable that you all get along so well together."

"All it takes is patience and love—and lots of prayer."

"Do you know where Damien is today?" Emma asked.

"He only said he had some business to take care of," Carolina said. "I promised to entertain you today, and I have some ideas for how to do that."

"That's not necessary. I can find plenty to do around here."

"Then do me a favor," Carolina said.

"If I can."

"Get me out of the house. Join me for lunch and then I'll take you and Belle on a drive around the area. I'll show you the school where all my sons went, and then if we have time, I'll show you where we attend church."

"I'd love that, but I don't have an infant seat for Belle."

"You do now. I had a friend pick one up for me when she was in town yesterday."

"Then I accept your offer."

"Great. Why don't we plan to leave here about eleven-thirty."

"I'll be ready."

But not eager. Emma was growing weary of playing the role she'd assigned to herself and sick of having to lie to Carolina. She couldn't go on like this much longer, especially when her leaving was inevitable. Today might offer the perfect opportunity to ask Carolina if she'd take on the task of finding Belle's father.

Then Emma would just disappear the way she'd always planned. Damien wouldn't understand or like it, but it would be the best thing Emma could do for him.

She'd give that serious thought and work out the details while she dressed.

Emma looked down at Belle and wrapped her hand

around a kicking foot. Leaving Belle and Damien might be the toughest thing she'd ever had to do.

She owed that to Caudillo, too.

IF THERE HAD BEEN DOUBT about Carolina's sphere of influence reaching all the way to the social heights of the Dallas community, it was dispelled within minutes of reaching the Beth's Café where they went for lunch.

They'd barely sat down when a smartly coiffed middle-age woman wearing an expensive-looking gray-and-black suit joined them. She dropped a newspaper on the table and tapped the photo at the top of the society page.

"Did you see this, Carolina?"

"I noticed the picture at breakfast."

Emma leaned over for a closer look. The woman in the sleek red ball gown was obviously Carolina. She checked out the caption: Governor Miller and Carolina Lambert Cut the Ribbon for the Groundbreaking of the New Lambert Wing at Children's Hospital in Dallas.

"So is it true?" the woman insisted.

Carolina replied, "It's true the governor and I cut the ribbon, Mary Anne. You knew the wing was being planned."

"I'm not talking about the hospital wing. That's old hat. I'm talking about you and the governor being an item."

"An item? You've lost me."

Mary Anne started tapping again. "Elisha mentions right here in her article that you and the governor made a dashing couple dancing at the ball that followed."

"We danced once. And it wasn't exactly a ball. It was a money-raising event for the hospital. Now sit down and let me introduce you to my houseguest."

Mary Anne looked at Emma as if she'd just realized she was there.

"Emma, this is one of my best friends—who has a terrible habit of believing all the gossip she hears and then spreading it around as fast as she can."

"Governor Miller is very nice looking. Even you have to admit that, Carolina," Mary Anne said in her defense.

"And there are plenty of women who would love to be linked with him. I'm not one of them. Mary Anne, this is Emma Smith. And the adorable cherub in her arms is Belle."

"I'm pleased to meet you," she said, offering a hand and then doing her version of coochie-coo to Belle. "I didn't know you were having guests this week."

"It was a surprise visit."

Mary Anne pursed her lips. "I'd love to stay longer, but I want to do some shopping before the symphony board meeting tonight. I'll see you there."

"Not tonight," Carolina said. "I canceled, but everyone already knows I favor continuing the free concerts for school children throughout the year."

"Then I guess I'll catch you later in the week. Nice to meet you, Emma. Your daughter is adorable."

Mary Anne's heels clicked on the slate floor as she left.

"Do you get the feeling a whirlwind just went through?" Carolina said.

"Definitely, but she seems nice."

"She's a great friend, one who was there for me after Hugh's death. She just tends to get caught up in the gossip of the moment."

"You do lead a very busy life," Emma said. "I'm afraid having Belle and me around has really inconvenienced you."

"Not for a minute. I've made myself stay busy since Hugh's death, but for the most part that's all it is. Just activities to keep me from drowning in grief. Having you and Belle around has been a blessing."

"I'm glad you feel that way because—"

Her words were interrupted by the young waitress, who seemed to pop up from thin air. "I'm sorry I took so long, Mrs. Lambert. That party of twelve on the far side of the room walked in just before you did and they had questions about every item on the menu."

"No problem. Is Beth around?"

"She had an appointment in Dallas this morning, but she'll be in later today. Is there something I can help you with?"

"No, I just wanted to tell her hello and to introduce her to my houseguest."

Instead she introduced Emma and Belle to the waitress. Emma let Carolina do the ordering for them. She took that opportunity to look around the restaurant.

Almost all of the tables were taken and several people were walking around in the gift section to the left of the tables. Most of the items that she could see from her chair seemed to fit into a kitchen theme. They were all unusual and eye-catching.

"Oak Grove must be larger than I thought," Emma said as the waitress walked away. "I wouldn't have thought it would support a café and gift shop as nice as this one."

"You'd be amazed at how many ranching families live in the area. They spread out in every direction. Many are small ranches used by Dallasites as weekend homes. Several of the bigger ranches are owned by professional ball players and even movie stars who like owning a ranch where they can escape the hassles of fame. Most are just small ranchers doing what they love."

"But none are as large as Bent Pine Ranch?"

"Not in this part of the state. Living on a ranch has a lot to offer, Emma."

"I'm sure it does."

"Damien loves it. I can't see him living anywhere but on the ranch, but I wish he'd find the right woman and fall in love. I may be slightly prejudiced, but I think he'd make a terrific husband and father." Carolina smiled mischievously. "And from a selfish standpoint, I'm ready for grandkids."

This was not the direction Emma had planned for the conversation to go. If she was going to say anything, she'd best say it now.

Belle vetoed that by beginning to fuss.

"She's probably getting hungry," Carolina said. "Why don't you let me feed her so that you can enjoy your lunch when it comes?"

"But then you won't get to eat yours."

"That's okay. Feeding Belle is much more of a treat for me."

Maybe this was the time to say what was on her mind. She handed Belle off to Carolina and took the bottle from the oversize handbag Carolina had insisted she borrow.

"I can see how fond you are of Belle," she said. "I know this may sound like an imposition, but—"

The waitress returned with their drinks. Before she left them, a middle-age woman walked through the door, waved to Carolina and headed straight to their table.

The favor Emma needed to ask would just have to wait. But some things couldn't. A new plan began to formulate in her mind.

Chapter Twelve

There was no sign of Damien when Emma and Carolina returned to the ranch. But the drive had given Emma time to do some serious thinking. She couldn't go on like this.

She was falling in love with Damien. And Carolina was starting to visualize her as a daughter-in-law.

But nothing had really changed with Caudillo. She might feel safe on the ranch. Damien might keep reassuring her she was safe. But Caudillo would not have given up.

She picked up the phone in her bedroom and punched in the number for her former office in Nashville.

"Dorothy Paul, please," she requested when the receptionist answered.

"Could you repeat that?"

"Dorothy Paul. She's a tech agent."

"Dorothy Paul is no longer with the Bureau. May I direct your call to someone else?"

"No. Wait. Am I talking to Sally Jenkins?"

"Yes. Who is this?"

She hesitated, but she'd reached desperation level. She had to know if Dorothy was alive. "It's Emma Muran, Sally. Long time, huh?"

"Girl, is it ever? How in the world are you? You're still married, aren't you?"

"How did you hear about that?"

"From everybody. Well, from Dorothy first, of course, but then from Arnold Sawyer when you turned in your resignation. You go on vacation and wind up married to a billionaire with a mansion in the Caribbean. I was sick with envy. Does he have a brother?"

"No brother." Emma's mind reeled as if she'd been dropped into another dimension. "I've been trying to get in touch with Dorothy. Do you know how I can reach her?"

"You know she quit right after you did, don't you?"

"No, we kind of lost touch after I left Nashville."

"You're kidding. You haven't heard her good news?"

"No, did she get a promotion?"

"Way better than that. She won a lottery—the Florida one, I think. Not one of the super jackpots, but enough that she quit work and moved to Oregon. You two became the big motto around here."

"What motto was that?"

"Go to Work for the Nashville ATF and Get Rich. I'm still waiting."

"Do you think anyone around there has a phone number or an address for her? Even a city would help."

"I seriously doubt it. Dorothy just came whirling in one morning, tossed a handful of hundred-dollar bills in the air like they were confetti and told us all she was moving to Oregon."

"Why Oregon?"

"She didn't say, and it all happened so fast no one thought to ask. You can imagine how pissed Sawyer was, losing two tech agents in a matter of days and neither of you giving notice."

"Is Sawyer still there?"

"Yeah. And as standoffish as ever with us lowlifes who only work for him. He's been away on some secret project for the last two weeks, but he's due back in the office tomorrow if you want to give him a call and see if he knows how to reach Dorothy. My guess is that he doesn't."

"I might do that. Any other big news in the department?"

"Kevin Greene and his wife got divorced. Mary Nell is pregnant. And I have a new pair of Jimmy Choo boots that I practically had to mortgage the house to pay for. I think that's it."

"Then I should let you get back to work."

"What? No invite to visit you in paradise? That smarts."

"Paradise is grossly overrated."

THE TUESDAY EVENING MEAL at Bent Pine Ranch was served at the dining room table rather than in the kitchen. The menu consisted of homemade chicken enchiladas, black beans, the best flan Emma had ever tasted and enough tension to choke one of Damien's bulls.

Carolina hadn't been the cook. Apparently a middle-age Hispanic woman named Alda with a flair for the delicious and a lyrical laugh did the kitchen chores Monday through Friday.

Alda didn't eat with the family, but her congenial manner made her seem more like a friend than a servant. She kidded around with Pearl as she served and cooed at Belle, fortunately rescuing them all from what would have been a series of awkward silences, interrupted only by the sound of chewing.

Even Belle was fussier than usual, not crying but whimpering and squirming as if something hurt. Emma held her in every position she could think of to no avail.

Emma hadn't had the opportunity to be alone with Damien since her talk with Carolina. But sitting across the table from him now, she could tell he was upset. Emma was certain it concerned her.

As for Carolina, her eyes were red and slightly swollen. Emma figured she'd had a grief meltdown. The seeds for that had been sown while she was showing Emma the family chapel where they'd been married. It was on the ranch itself but easily accessible by car.

Even Tague was unusually quiet. Sybil was missing in action, having gone into the city to meet a friend for dinner.

It was hard to believe this was the same jovial family she'd interrupted at mealtime just a few nights ago.

Enter Emma Muran and everyone's world turned dark. She felt like the comic-book character with the rain cloud over his head.

"If you'll excuse us, I need to steal Emma away for a bit," Damien said as soon as the dessert plates were cleared away.

"Let me take Belle for you," Carolina volunteered.

"It's my turn to rock her," Pearl announced. "You've been hogging that baby ever since she got here. I s'pect what she needs is a grandma's touch. The rest of you just scoot on out of here."

"A grandma's touch is probably exactly what she needs," Emma agreed.

"Why don't you go claim your choice of back-porch rockers," Carolina said, "and I'll bring Belle to you."

"And find some George Strait music on that i-thingy you're always listening to, Carolina. What this house needs is music."

"You're right," Carolina said. "I'll get the iPod dock and put on something to cheer us up."

Damien turned to Emma. "Do you mind grabbing that

jacket Mother lent you so that we can go for a walk? I think better when I'm moving."

"A walk is fine. In fact, you may want me to just keep walking after you hear what I found out this afternoon."

"I'll be at headquarters if you want to get together later," Tague said.

"Give me an hour," Damien replied.

Something was rotten in Denmark. Emma zipped the borrowed parka and followed Damien out the door.

DAMIEN LED EMMA TO THE old tire swing that hung from a branch of an oak about thirty yards beyond the swimming pool. He'd spent a lot of time there when he was a kid, pumping that old tire as high as he could go and then jumping to the ground.

All his friends had fancy swing sets in their yards. Damien had asked for one, but his dad had refused to let him have it. He'd claimed they stifled the imagination and limited a kid's fun and spirit of adventure. He'd said that about a lot of things that other kids had and Damien didn't. Damien was grown before he realized his dad had been right.

He didn't know why he was thinking about that now except that he needed a big dose of imagination to figure out where to go from here. He'd spent the day getting more information to back up or deny the bad news he'd gotten after returning from their flight to the Caribbean.

Nothing of what he learned was in Emma's favor.

"Sit on the tire," he said, acting on a sudden burst of inspiration.

"I'd rather stand."

"Sit on the tire, please."

"You asked me out here to talk."

"I know, but for what I have to say, we need clear heads

and a bit more optimism than either of us is exhibiting right now."

She eased onto the tire.

"Now pick up your feet and hold on tight." He grabbed the edge of the rim, pulled the tire back and then heaved it forward. Emma went flying through the air as he'd done at age seven or eight when the worst problems he'd had to deal with were multiplication and reprimands for talking in class.

He pushed her higher and higher until her feet were almost skimming the low-hanging branches of the tree, and she squealed like a schoolgirl. Finally, he let it slow on its own. Just before it stopped completely, he caught her outstretched hands and pulled her into his arms.

She held on tight for long moments, and he could feel the pounding of her heart against his chest. It took all his willpower to let go of her.

"What was that about?" she asked.

"Life, freedom and the pursuit of happiness. Now you go first. What do you need to tell me?"

"Let's walk," she said.

He took her hand as they strolled in the moonlight. They might have been mistaken for carefree lovers by someone too far away to hear the strain in Emma's voice.

He paid close attention to her recounting her conversation with the receptionist where she'd once worked, though nothing she said shocked him tonight.

"We both know it's unlikely Dorothy just happened to win the lottery the same month I was kidnapped," Emma said.

"Highly unlikely," he agreed.

"Do you think it's possible she was in on this with Caudillo from the beginning?"

"I know it's hard to accept that a woman you thought of

as a good friend could turn on you," he said. "But, yeah, I think there's a good chance she sold you out."

"Then she couldn't have understood the full extent of what she was doing. I can't accept that she'd knowingly put me through anything that heinous."

"I guess we'll never know."

"I refuse to settle for that, Damien. I know I was the one who wanted to run from everything in the beginning, but not anymore. I intend to find Dorothy and talk to her face-to-face. I want her to hear what every day of my life was like locked away with a monster."

He loved the fight in Emma and hated that he was going to have to steal if from her. He tugged her to a stop and took both of her hands in his.

"I know where Dorothy is, Emma, but talking to her may not get you anywhere."

"Where is she?"

"In a Portland nursing home."

"Why? What happened to her?"

"Three months after you were kidnapped, a neighbor found her slumped over the wheel of her new luxury car in the closed garage of her new Oregon home. The carbon monoxide poisoning left her with severe brain damage.

"Reportedly, she has occasional lucid moments, but most of the time she just repeats nonsensical phrases."

Emma tensed and pulled away. "She must have realized what she'd done to me and tried to kill herself."

"Seems if she'd been that upset, she'd have just gone to the authorities and had them rescue you."

"So you don't believe she tried to kill herself?"

"I'm not convinced of it," Damien said.

"You think Caudillo tried to kill her?"

"Him or someone he'd hired to do it."

"As punishment because she'd misled him," Emma said,

catching on fast. "She told him I could get him access to secret files when I couldn't. And then she got me to the Caribbean and Misterioso Island to make it easy for him to kidnap me. And I played into the scheme without missing a cue."

"You trusted Dorothy."

"I'd still like to see her, Damien. Maybe seeing me will jolt some part of her brain that's not as damaged as they think. But I don't expect you to take more time off from the ranch to fly me out there. I can do that much on my own."

"And you'd be playing right into Caudillo's hands again."

"I don't see how."

"Think about it. She was your best friend. He'd expect you to look her up and then try to see her."

"Do you have a better idea?"

"I'm working on one, but you have to make some modifications to our original agreement."

"Such as?"

"I need to tell Tague and Durk everything. I need the help of people I can trust, and there's no one alive I trust more than my brothers."

"If they're smart, they'll tell you to kick me out of your life and forget Caudillo."

"Not a chance, not once they know the whole truth. They'll say it's time to kick butt and take the low-down kidnapping, woman-torturing arms dealer down. Of course, they'll throw in a few additional descriptive adjectives."

"It would be a lot simpler and safer for all of you if I just walk out of your life."

"You know, if you keep threatening to run away from

me, I'm going to develop a complex. Next thing I know you'll be vomiting on me."

"Not unless you spin me instead of swing me in that tire."

"Right now, I just need you to give me some time. Go back inside and don't mention any of this to Mother, Grandma or Sybil when she gets home. There's no need to alarm them."

"Aren't you coming in?"

"Not yet. I'll be in the office with Tague in a phone conference with Durk. He's waiting on my call."

"Does that mean you've already told them everything?"

"No, but I'd planned to tell them tonight whether you agreed or not. Caudillo has got to be stopped, and you deserve to get your life back without living in the shadow of fear."

"Okay. Tell them what you want, Damien. But if they just want me off the ranch, I want you to tell me that."

"I promise, but that's not going to happen." He touched his lips to hers, just one sweet taste, but the thrill raced through him.

"And the sooner you get your life back, the sooner I get to see you in—or out of—that hot-pink nightie. Before you drive me out of my mind."

CAUDILLO STRETCHED OUT ON the bed in his room at the New Orleans Ritz-Carlton. It wasn't quite as luxurious as his bedroom on the yacht, but the yacht was speeding toward Rio de Janeiro without him. All according to plan.

His warehouse on the island was cleared of all traces of weapons and instead stocked full of cashew nuts. He didn't have to worry about Emma's DNA being on any surface in the house or gardens. After all, she was his wife, though she'd chosen to leave him.

He reached for the room service menu and searched until he found a seafood dish that titillated his taste buds. Life was good.

He'd take care of Emma and then he'd finish off Dorothy Paul, as well. Though he had to admit that the failed attempt on her life that he'd orchestrated and paid for had given him immense satisfaction. A giant joke after she'd been so thrilled with his original payoff. But she shouldn't have lied and made him think that Emma had more clout than she did.

His cell phone vibrated. He picked it up from the bedside table. "You're calling late. You must have news."

"I know where you can find Emma Muran."

Chapter Thirteen

"Damn," Durk said. "When you said Emma was in serious danger, I figured it was something like writing bad checks or lying to the Mexican police. I never dreamed you were talking about evil that spanned continents and threatens national security."

"Right," Tague agreed. "If those weapons are getting into the hands of the drug cartels, it's bad enough. They might be going straight to terrorist organizations buying our weapons illegally to use against us."

"Add that to kidnapping, torturing and killing women, and you're looking the devil in the face straight on," Durk said.

"What worries me the most," Damien said, "is that Caudillo always seems to be one step ahead of the game, like filing that marriage license. And I'm sure he's behind Dorothy Paul's brain damage."

"I'd have to agree with that," Durk said. "Whether it was payback or to make sure she didn't talk, it proves what he's capable of doing to avoid getting caught."

"I say turn it over to the FBI and let them call the shots," Tague said. "Our concentration can be on keeping Emma safe."

"I don't know," Durk said. "I keep thinking about the women he kidnapped and killed. There could be dozens of them. Every one of them someone's daughter or sister or wife. Maybe even a mother."

"It would be a lot less complicated if he was operating from inside the United States," Damien said. "But once the arms are smuggled out of the country, things get sticky. Even if the FBI can put together enough solid evidence to arrest him based on Emma's testimony, it could take months for them to get to him with all the rules and regulations they'd have to follow."

"If we knew he was holding an American citizen hostage now, things could be expedited," Durk said, "but as far as we know, that's not the case."

"You're right," Tague said. "But if we're talking about waiting months, who knows how many women he might have kidnapped by then?"

"Damien, you've been working on this for a few days," Durk said. "You must have some ideas about how to proceed from here."

"I've given this a lot of thought," Damien said. "Caudillo is smart. There's no doubt about that. We have to be smarter."

"And you have a plan?" Tague asked.

"Based on what I've seen and heard, I think Caudillo was telling the truth about having friends in high places. It explains how he's kept operating so long. I have a strong hunch that one of his sources is with the Nashville ATF office. That's likely how he found out that it was Dorothy and not Emma who'd lied about what security-protected files Emma could access. At the time Emma was kidnapped, Caudillo's source might have even believed she had more clearance than she did since they worked in different departments."

"Do you have a suspect?" Durk asked.

"No, but I think if it's leaked to the media that the arrest of an ATF agent in that office is imminent, the traitorous bastard may out himself."

"I'm not following you," Durk said.

"I think I am," Tague said, "and I like it. The guilty agent will know that Caudillo's not going to risk getting outed by his source, a man who'll have all the scoop on him. So he'll bolt or possibly become so desperate that he does something to give himself away. He may even turn himself in before Caudillo has him taken out."

"Either way, once he's identified, the authorities can offer him protection in exchange for his help in leading Caudillo into a trap," Damien said. "I admit it's a long shot, but it could work. I just haven't figured out how to handle the details yet."

"Your only chance of getting it to work is to persuade the ATF or some other government agency to work with us on this," Durk said. "Tell you what, I have a very good friend with the CIA, Jerry Delaney, who I know I can trust. Why don't I give him a call in the morning, pick his brain and get back to you?"

"That'll work," Damien said. "But be sure he knows we're dealing with a psychopath, and under no circumstances do I want Emma involved in his capture or anything said publicly that could lead Caudillo to the Bent Pine."

"Don't worry. I have family there, remember? In fact, I think it's time you hire protection for the ranch. If Caudillo is as smart as he seems, he's out gathering information and making plans the same as you."

"I'll take care of that first thing in the morning. And thanks, guys. I knew I could count on you for support."

"That's what brothers are for, but bear in mind that I can't make Delaney do anything he doesn't agree to. We just have to hope he and the department see it our way."

EMMA SAT ON THE EDGE OF the bed, watching Belle as she slept in the same cradle that Damien had once slept in. So sweet and innocent.

Emma trailed a finger down Belle's soft cheek. "Your mother loved you very much, little princess. I wish you could always know that. Maybe I'll find you one day when you're old enough to understand and tell you how much she loved you."

Emma stood and walked to the window. She had no idea why the aching sense of loss that had haunted her through much of her childhood was surging so strong tonight.

Her growing attachment to Belle likely had something to do with it. So did watching Carolina's face as she'd adoringly held the picture of Damien and his father.

Or maybe it was just a factor of the emotional turmoil that had started churning inside her the night she was kidnapped and that had refused to settle down. How could it, when Caudillo still controlled her life? Not only hers now, but Damien's, as well.

She hated Caudillo with a fierceness that she'd never known existed until she'd endured his mental torture month after month after agonizing month.

Now she was dwelling on that hate, when love was all around her. Carolina brought that to this family.

Carolina's words played in her mind like a sweet country ballad.

Choose love, Emma. Always choose love.

Even without promises of forever, the words made sense. Not to choose love was letting priceless moments of life slip away.

Emma had already lost too many moments to waste a single one now, but how could she move on when her fear of Caudillo refused to let go of her?

DAMIEN STAYED OUTSIDE FOR at least a half hour after Tague went in. He liked the sounds on the ranch at night. The hoot of an owl. The rustling in the grass made by a family of skunks out searching for food. The croak of a bullfrog in the nearby pond. The scratching of an armadillo in the rich earth beneath the shrubs.

The only illumination in the back of the house when he finally went inside was the dim glow of the under-counter lights that they frequently left on all night. Damien walked to the counter and reached for a water glass.

"What's wrong, Damien?"

He turned at his mother's voice. She was sitting alone at the kitchen table.

"Nothing's wrong. What are you doing sitting in here by yourself this late?"

"Thinking about you and the worry I read in your face. I know this has to do with Emma. It started when she arrived. Is she in some kind of trouble?"

"Nothing you don't know about."

"Julio's death was ruled self-defense. But the two of you are more anxious than ever."

She'd always been able to see through his lies. No use to try. He'd just have to soft-pedal the truth. He took his glass of water to the table and straddled a chair.

"Emma's working through some issues from the past, but she's making progress. I'm just trying to help her look at some options for dealing with obstacles."

"What kind of issues?"

"An abusive relationship."

"Is she still in danger from this man?"

"She could be. That's why I've asked her to stay on here, but don't worry. I plan to hire additional protection so none of you will be in danger."

"I can't imagine the man would be foolish enough to

show up here with you, Tague and all the wranglers we have around. But if I can help with anything, let me know."

"I'd appreciate it if you wouldn't broach the subject with Emma. If you do, she's liable to just run away again and then she might be in real danger."

"I'll take my cues from you. I like Emma. She's easy to talk to, and I love the way she's bonded with Belle."

"I like her, too, Mother. I like her a lot."

He reached for a snapshot lying at his mother's elbow and held it up so that he could see it in the dim light. "This is an old picture. Who's that Dad's bathing?"

"You."

"I'm smiling big, but Dad looks like he's in pain."

"You'd just splashed water all over him and he was grumbling like a bear. I was laughing so hard I could barely focus the camera, but it's always been one of my favorites."

"Grumbling like a bear, huh? So even as a baby I had that effect on him."

"We all had that effect on him at times."

"But no one was as good at it as me."

"That's not true. Your father pushed you too hard at times, but he was always proud of you, Damien."

The question of the birth certificate niggled Damien's thoughts. This was probably as good a time as any to deal with it. "I have a question for you, Mother."

"You can ask me anything."

"Who was Damien Briggs?"

"Is this some kind of game? Because I'm not sure I'm up to a brain teaser tonight."

"It's not a game. When I was getting the boxes you wanted down from the attic the other day, I saw a birth certificate for a Damien Briggs. His birthday was the same as mine, but the name of the mother was Melissa Briggs."

She winced as if he'd slapped her. "You must have read it wrong."

"I read it exactly as it was printed. The line for the father's name was blank."

Carolina started to rub her arms nervously. His uneasiness swelled to a strangling knot in his gut. "I'm not really your son, am I?"

Carolina buried her face in her hands.

"I guess that's my answer." He started to stand up, but she grabbed his arm and held on, digging her fingernails into his flesh.

"You're my son in every way that matters, Damien. I didn't give birth to you, but I loved you from the first second I saw you. I built my life around you. No mother could love a biological son more than I love you. Surely you know that."

Tears slid from her eyes and wet her cheeks. He should say something to comfort her, but those words wouldn't come. "What happened to my real mother?"

"I'm your real mother, do you hear me, Damien? I'm your mother and always will be."

"What happened to Melissa Briggs?"

"It was so long ago, Damien. Does it really matter now?"

"It matters to me."

"Then I guess I'll have to start with the beginning." She took a deep breath and exhaled slowly.

"I've never talked much about my family because there never seemed a reason to, but you have to know some of our background to understand my sister, Melissa."

"Go back as far as you need to."

"Our mother dropped us off at my grandmother's when I was ten and Melissa was twelve. She never came back to pick us up. We learned later that she'd died of a drug overdose."

"Where was your father?"

"I never met him, never knew his name. Mother cut us off quickly whenever either Melissa or I asked about him. Anyway, Grandma did the best she could to take care of Melissa and me, but she had no money and problems of her own."

"What kind of problems?"

"The doctor called it chronic depression, but looking back I think there may have been a personality disorder or two in there, as well. So Melissa and I basically raised ourselves.

"Melissa had a much harder time than I did, probably because she was the oldest. Anyway, I was the student. She was the wild child. I got a scholarship to UT and earned a degree in premed. She went to New Orleans and got a job as an exotic dancer."

"But you didn't become a doctor."

"No. I became a mother."

"And Melissa?"

"Got mixed up with the wrong crowd in New Orleans. I was preparing to start med school when I got word that she and her boyfriend had been shot while robbing a liquor store. The cops found you in the backseat of the getaway car. You were four weeks old at the time, about the same age as Belle is now."

"So you and Dad adopted me?"

"Hugh wasn't in the picture then. I went to the funeral and the social worker laid you in my arms. I'll never forget that moment. It was like you crawled inside my heart. You were as much a part of me as the blood that ran through my veins. You still are, Damien."

"A part of you, maybe, but I'm not Hugh's flesh and blood. He was stuck with me to marry you."

"That's not true, Damien, and don't call your father Hugh. He was your daddy. He's the one who was determined you not know that you were adopted because he never wanted you to feel different from your brothers. You were our son in his mind."

"I'm not a Lambert."

"You're every bit as much a part of this family as Tague and Durk."

"You should have told me the truth. You should have told me long before now."

"Your father and I may have made a mistake in judgment, son, but not with our hearts. We always gave you all the love we had to give. If that's not enough, I don't know what else to say."

Neither did Damien. He was numb…staggered…empty inside.

All his life he'd been a Lambert.

All his life had been a lie.

He walked away without saying a word, knowing his mother was hurting and unable to offer her anything. His muscles ached from a debilitating fatigue he hadn't noticed earlier. But instead of going to his room, he found himself at Emma's door.

He knocked once and then stepped inside. She was stretched out between the sheets, but she sat up when he entered. The room was dark, but silvery moonlight caressed her face, making her look like an angelic illusion.

"I didn't know you'd already gone to bed."

But she took one look at him and then opened her arms and beckoned him inside.

Chapter Fourteen

Only then did he come to his senses and pull away. It was not the time for this. Not yet. Not when he was dealing with his own frustrations and her life was in turmoil.

"You look upset," Emma said. "It's Caudillo, isn't it? What now?"

"It's nothing to do with Caudillo," he said, wondering why he'd come in here in the first place. She certainly didn't need to wrestle with his problems.

"Sit down." She patted the side of the bed next to her. He sat, but couldn't bring himself to meet her penetrating gaze.

"I just came in to say good-night, but I don't want to wake Belle."

"You're a poor liar, Damien. What happened? And don't worry. As long as we keep our voices low, we won't wake Belle. Fortunately, she's not a light sleeper."

"Family problems. No use for you to get involved."

"So my problems are an open book but yours are off-limits?"

"I didn't mean it that way." Sharing gut-wrenching emotions had never come easy for him. But instead of leaving, he lay down beside her, put his hands behind his head and stared at the ceiling.

"I level with you," Emma said. "I feel a bit betrayed when you don't do the same with me."

Betrayed. That was exactly how he felt. Only, the betrayers had been the people he trusted most in the world.

"Okay," he said. "But remember, you asked for it." He repeated what he'd just heard from his mother, while he did his dead-level best to keep his anger and frustration in check. Emma listened without interruption until he grew quiet again.

"I can see how finding out you were adopted at this late date would be a shock," she offered.

"Shock is an understatement. I've gone through the first thirty years of my life believing I'm a Lambert. But I'm not."

"What are you talking about? They adopted you. Of course you're a Lambert."

"Legally, but being a Lambert means more than that. It's a bloodline. It's traditions and land and houses passed down through generations."

"It's being a member of the Lambert family," Emma said. "Your mother's a good example. Carolina isn't a Lambert by blood, yet she's the heart of the Lambert clan. You don't have to be in this house but a few minutes to realize that."

"That's different. Mother's practically a saint. I'm…I'm the son of a couple who were killed while robbing a liquor store."

"So? You just told me that Carolina's mother died of a drug overdose. I haven't noticed Carolina sniffing any white powder. Like you said, she's practically a saint."

"You don't get it, Emma. I'm not who I thought I was. Tague and Durk are Lamberts. I'm the cheap imitation."

"Nothing about you is cheap, Damien."

"You know what I mean."

"Not exactly. Are you telling me that if by some weird stretch of the imagination you and I got married and adopted Belle, she wouldn't be a Lambert? She'd be kicked out of the traditions and not allowed to do things like wear your mother's wedding dress or inherit Sybil's wig?"

"She can't inherit the wig. It's going to the grave with Aunt Sybil. But you know that Belle would become an integral part of the family. She practically is already."

"Exactly."

"*Not* exactly. The truth is there was always a wedge between Hugh and me. He was harder on me than he ever was on Durk or Tague. I didn't understand it growing up, but it makes sense now. Hugh never saw me as his son."

"Now it's 'Hugh'?"

"Okay, my adopted father never saw me as his son."

"Maybe not, but nothing you've said proves that to me. Most men treat first sons differently than their younger brothers. One of my psychology professors said that men look for images of themselves in the firstborn. When they see their own faults, they feel compelled to make sure their sons overcome them. They relax more with the sons who are born after that."

"Nice in theory."

"Want to hear about my family?"

"Have we run out of every topic under the sun?"

"No, but I think it's time you know what kind of stock I come from, since you're into that kind of superficiality. When I was six years old, my mother called me into the living room and announced to me and my father that she needed time to go and find herself.

"I thought we were talking about a game of hide-and-seek until she brought out the luggage and kissed me goodbye and said she didn't know when she'd be back. I stood at the door screaming for her not to leave me. That's one of the most vivid memories of my childhood."

"Did she find herself?"

"No, but she found Jim the barber, Raphael the tennis pro and Simon the hairdresser. I could go on."

"You met all of these lovers?"

"No, but my father told me about them so that I would be sure to know that my mother was a tramp. Then one day he proved how noble he was by not coming home from work. Not ever coming home again."

"What happened to him?"

"No one knows. Looking back, I suspect he got tired of being a father the way my mother had gotten tired of being a mother. I began my tour of foster homes."

"You seem to have done a great job of moving past all of that."

"I handle it well now—for the most part. At age six, it devastated me. Fortunately, at age eleven I ended up with the smartest and most caring foster mother a girl could ever wish for. She turned my life around and helped me crawl out from under the shell built by the cutting sands of rejection."

"I'm glad you left your shell."

"I left that one. Now I'm working on the one that Caudillo buried me under. But I'm making progress. Thanks to the Lamberts—one Lambert in particular." She snuggled against him, and his will to fight his feelings for her grew weaker. He ached to make love to her, but he wouldn't. Not until the time was right and Caudillo was out of her life for good. For now, he'd have to be satisfied with holding her close.

He was a long way from making peace with the fact

that he was not Carolina and Hugh's son. But he had Emma in his arms and Caudillo on his radar.

He'd deal with the rest in time.

IT WAS NINE IN THE MORNING and Damien had just finished going over the day's work schedule with his crew of wranglers when he got a call from Durk.

"I'm surprised to hear from you this early. I know you haven't had time to meet with Delaney yet."

"Actually, we met at eight for coffee."

"Had Delaney ever heard of Caudillo?"

"Oh, yeah. He says the compound on Enmascarado Island has been raided twice in the past five years. Both times they worked with Caribbean officials. Once, the on-site warehouse was filled with bananas. The second time, it was stacked high with burlap bags of cashew nuts."

"So he obviously was expecting them. How did Delaney react to my suspicions that someone in the ATF is responsible for the leaks?"

"He was open to the possibility. They've currently moved their focus to stopping Caudillo from getting his hands on the weapons in the first place, rather than apprehending him with the goods."

"That's obviously not working for them, either."

"Delaney acknowledged that."

"What about the kidnappings? Have they investigated those?"

"I know you don't want to hear this, Damien, but Delaney was skeptical about the kidnapping claim, especially after I'd told him about the marriage license."

"Emma's telling the truth."

"In your opinion. Delaney sees it from a different perspective. He says Caudillo is known worldwide as a playboy, and women flock to him. He has a yacht. He has money. And according to Delaney he's a sophisticated charmer."

"That's pretty much the reaction I expected," Damien said, "and the reason I didn't go straight to the CIA or the FBI with this myself."

"The good news is that Delaney liked your idea pretty much just as you outlined it. Now the challenge is getting clearance to put it into action."

"I hope they're careful with the wording of the leak. Caudillo is crafty. You don't want him figuring out this is a trap."

"Do you have a wording suggestion?"

"Something like, 'Unsubstantiated reports indicate that an ATF official in the Nashville office will be charged within the next day or two with unethical behavior that may have led to countless deaths along our southern borders.'"

"That may be too vague," Durk said.

"I don't think so. Caudillo will get the message and so will his source, and they're the only ones we're targeting."

"Good point. Let Tague know where we are on this."

"Will do. Did Delaney give you odds on whether or not his plan would be approved?"

"He says it's a long shot, so don't start thinking of it as a done deal. They've already extended a lot of manpower and expense on apprehending Caudillo with no positive results."

"This time could be the charm." Damien was counting on it.

When the conversation was finished, he made a call to the same security agency he'd used two years ago when Carolina had received a couple of threatening letters. Turned out they had been from a harmless crackpot in Dallas who had opposing political views.

But the company had done a great job of covering the ranch with a protective net of agents. Not that his wranglers weren't crack shots. And they carried guns with them for protection against copperheads and water moccasins.

At this point, there was no reason to suspect Caudillo knew that Emma was at Bent Pine or connected with him in any way. But with things heating up, Damien would leave nothing to chance.

"YOU HAVE TO WASH UNDER her chin, Damien. Just move her head so that you can. She won't break."

"She's got three chins. Which one do I get under?"

"All of them."

Giving Belle a bath proved to be more than Damien bargained for. Now he just wanted it over. "Do you think she actually needs a bath? It's not like she's been playing in the dirt."

"No, but she poops and urinates and spits up. And think of all the hands that touch her during the day."

"But she's so slippery when she's wet and soapy. What if she slides from your hands while I'm doing the washing?"

"She won't. Oops, you missed under her arms."

"C'mon. I know she hasn't been sweating. It's January."

"I think you're afraid of Belle, Damien."

"I am. She wiggles and squirms and kicks, and her head's not screwed on tight. Every time I hold her, I'm afraid I'll let something fall I'm supposed to be holding up."

"She's fragile but not that fragile." Emma's smile gave him a bit of moral support.

"Have you heard anything from the detective who's searching for Belle's father?" she asked, switching topics.

"Not since our trip to Fort Worth."

"I wonder how long children's services will let Belle stay here if we don't find her father."

"Won't they just leave her until we call and say come get her?"

"Hardly. Not without paperwork. Babies don't go by the finders-keepers rule, Damien. And they're not like an unbranded calf. I strongly suspect your mother has been pulling strings to keep her here this long."

"But Belle's fine here. It's not like she's homeless," Damien protested.

"Officially, she is. I'm sure there's some kind of time restriction on how long she can stay with us before she goes into foster care."

"Now, that makes a lot of sense. Take her away from this home, where she has a houseful of honorary grandmas, great-aunts and uncles, only to have to go searching for another family to take her in."

"That's government agencies for you." Emma lifted Belle from the baby tub of water and held her while Damien unfolded the towel and wrapped it around her dripping body.

Damien's cell phone rang. He checked the ID, hoping it was Durk with word from Delaney. The number came up as unavailable.

"Hello."

"I'm calling to talk to my wife. Is Emma there?"

Chapter Fifteen

Damien took the phone and walked out of Emma's earshot. "Who the hell is this?"

"There's no need for rudeness. I just have a message for my wife."

"Let's hear it."

"Tell her I miss her and I hope she's thinking about all the lovely, romantic evenings we spent together. And that I plan to see her soon."

"You depraved son of a bitch. How dare you call here?"

"How dare you try to steal my wife?"

There was a click and then the line went dead.

Fury raged inside Damien. He didn't dare let Emma see him like this. She'd know right away that something had gone terribly wrong. He shoved the phone into his pocket and stamped out the back door.

The armed guard watching the back of the house from an inconspicuous spot looked up and nodded. Damien nodded back. He'd up the alert level when he calmed down enough to meet with the man in charge. But talking to Durk couldn't wait.

"The urgency just ratcheted up a dozen notches," he said when Durk answered the call.

"What happened?"

"Caudillo knows that Emma is with me." Damien filled him in. "Get in touch with Delaney. See where we stand."

"Okay, I'll get back to you right away and let you know what I find out."

Damien was talking to the head of the security agency when Durk called back.

"Okay, bro. I filled Delaney in about the call from Caudillo. I think that got his attention and convinced him that Caudillo may be in the States and not on his yacht, which is currently off the coast of South America. He called me back five minutes later. The plan is a go, but the CIA also wants a team in place at the Bent Pine."

Damien's stomach muscles unclenched for the first time since Caudillo's call. "Now you're talking. When?"

"Everything's going down immediately, but only if Emma agrees to the CIA's terms. They'll send a team out from Dallas to pick her up and hold her under their protection at a safe location until the danger has passed."

"I can keep her safe."

"Don't blow this whole operation because of one simple concession, Damien. If you want Caudillo, take the deal. Delaney doesn't think he'll actually show up at the ranch. If he were going to do that, he wouldn't have signaled his intentions with that phone call. He thinks it far more likely he'll silence his source and then just move on. After all, Caudillo neutralized a lot of the damage Emma could do to him with that marriage license. Now she's just an angry wife with no real proof. It's her word against his."

"In that case, Delaney shouldn't have any problem with me taking Emma away from the ranch and keeping her safe."

"Not going to happen. They don't want any family members on the ranch, either. You can all stay at my condo in Dallas."

"Great. Tague can drive the others to Dallas. I'm staying on the Bent Pine. If Caudillo shows up here, I plan to be part of the welcoming party."

"I told Delaney you'd insist on that. He didn't like it, but he gave in on that one point."

"I'll move part of the security staff I hired to the condo, as well," Damien said.

Adrenaline had Damien's heart pumping like crazy as he went to find Emma. She'd be upset that she was bringing danger to the ranch, but she'd go along with the CIA's plan as long as it meant Caudillo's reign of terror might just possibly be about to come to an end.

EMMA PLANTED KISSES ON Belle's sweet cheeks and the top of her head before she handed her to Carolina. The agents were waiting impatiently to take her off to a safe house.

"I don't understand half of what's going on," Carolina lamented, "but we'll take good care of Belle."

Emma hugged Carolina and then told the rest of the family goodbye, saving Damien for last.

She slipped into his arms. "I'd rather stay with you."

"I know, but this will all be over soon and then I'll hang around until you're sick of me."

"Be careful, Damien. Please, just be careful."

"Always."

"No heroics, cowboy."

"No heroics. The CIA is here to handle that."

He kissed her goodbye and then she stepped away and slid into the backseat of the black sedan.

She felt as if spiked bricks were being pushed into her chest as the car pulled away and headed down the ranch road, leaving Damien behind.

She'd known from the first she'd end up putting

Damien and his family in danger. No one ever won against Caudillo. No one ever would.

As IT TURNED OUT, BOTH Damien and Durk stayed at the ranch while Tague as the youngest drew condo security duty.

"I guess Delaney figured you needed to be here to keep me in line," Damien said as they saddled a couple of horses.

"No. I just made my point that the Lambert brothers always work as a team."

It had always been that way. But that was when Damien believed that he actually was a Lambert. He forced himself to push past the anger that lurked just beneath the surface of his control. "So what's going on with the Nashville end of the Caudillo operation?"

"No one in the Nashville office except the very highest in the pecking order knows anything about the operation," Durk said. "It's expected that when the leak hits the news networks sometime today, the office will be buzzing."

"Will Delaney be there?"

"He, a half-dozen agents and one of the muckety-mucks at the top will be in the security offices, where they can scan cameras set up in the halls. They'll be able to see anyone who comes and goes into any office."

They climbed into the saddles and let the horses gallop full speed before slowing them to a walk near Beaver Creek. The same spot where he'd found Emma on Friday night. Now he was waiting and praying that the monster she'd escaped actually would show up at Bent Pine Ranch. Damien had never killed a man before, but he was certain he could pull the trigger and put a bullet though Caudillo's heart if it came to that.

It was unlikely that it would. The CIA agent in charge

had ordered them to stay out of the way, but he had promised to alert them the second Caudillo was spotted at the ranch. If he was spotted.

"Thanks for hanging around," Damien said. "I'm glad for the company."

"One for all, and all for one. That's the Lambert code."

And there it was again. It was all about being a Lambert. Damien stared at the pastures that stretched out in front of him. Not just a ranch, but a legacy that should never have fallen to him. He could keep his silence about the issue no longer.

"I'm not actually a Lambert."

"I know what you mean," Durk said. "I'm ready to deny kin sometimes myself, and I'm only here weekends. Who's getting to you? Mother? Sybil? Grandmother?"

"I'm serious, Durk. I'm adopted."

"Right. And I'm running for president."

"I'm not joking."

Durk stared at him as if he'd grown horns and a tail.

Damien explained the situation, starting with finding the birth certificate on Friday evening. When he finished, they both set in silence for a good five minutes as the horses meandered along the banks of the creek.

"I had no idea," Durk admitted, the shock pulling troubled lines into his face. "But it doesn't really change anything."

"It does for me."

"It won't for any of the rest of us. You're my brother, just like Tague is. Nothing can change that."

"You have to admit it explains a few things, like why nothing I did was ever good enough for Dad. I wasn't his son."

"I think you're reading way too much into this, Damien."

"I don't."

"If Dad didn't think of you as his firstborn son, then how come as the firstborn, you get the house and the furnishings? Which means you're the one who passes on the traditions of Christmas in the big house and the family rodeos in the fall and hosting the annual football-kickoff weekend shindig. He'd never have left you that if he didn't consider you family."

"I'm sure Mother insisted."

"Even Mother didn't have that kind of influence over Dad."

"So let's just drop it," Damien said. "I have more important things on my mind now."

"Good idea," Durk agreed. "Let's go back to the house."

The house that shouldn't be Damien's, to wait for a dangerous madman who might never show. But even if he didn't, Damien wouldn't give up on finding him. He couldn't change his relationship with his father, but he would save Emma from Caudillo if it was the last thing he did.

CAUDILLO FLICKED OFF THE news and swerved to the far right lane before slowing and pulling onto the shoulder. Imminent arrest of an ATF agent—hours after he'd made the call to Bent Pine Ranch?

If they believed he was fool enough to walk into their ill-conceived trap, they were truly imbeciles. But their little ploy would scare that weasel-faced Arnold Sawyer. He was probably messing up a pair of perfectly good trousers at this very minute.

Caudillo took the untraceable phone from his pocket and made a necessary call.

In minutes he'd given the orders for an execution. It was

a shame he wouldn't get to perform the duties himself, but he had even more important arrangements to make.

If it weren't so easy, outwitting his opponents would be quite fun.

Chapter Sixteen

"Did you hear the news?"

Arnold Sawyer looked up from the report he'd been reading, removed his glasses and flashed his secretary a smile. "What news?"

"That someone in our office is going to be arrested for unethical behavior."

"Who's sleeping with whom now?"

"That would only be news around here, like getting that call from Emma Muran yesterday."

Arnold swallowed hard, almost choking on his own saliva. "You talked to Emma Muran?"

"No, but the receptionist did. It sounds as if the honeymoon is over for Emma and the billionaire playboy. But this is much bigger. Looks as if someone's been leaking information to the wrong person and he's about to get nailed."

Emma had escaped. Someone was about to be accused of leaking information. His hands grew clammy. His stomach began to roll. He was in deep trouble.

He forced himself to maintain a semblance of composure until his secretary closed the door. He had to get out of here fast. There wasn't even time to make sure he wasn't leaving behind any incriminating evidence.

Not that it mattered. He wouldn't be coming back here again.

He started for the door and then went back for his laptop. It had information he'd need.

His door opened again and before he could turn around it closed and he heard the lock click into place.

"Going somewhere, Sawyer?"

"Who are you?"

"A friend of a friend."

"How did you get in here?"

"It wasn't easy. You've caused quite a commotion around here today, but no one wanted to keep the soft-drink delivery man away."

"I didn't tell anyone anything. I swear I didn't. I did everything Caudillo ever asked me to do. Everything. I repaid him a thousand times over for paying for my daughter's operation."

"Okay. Calm down and go back to your desk. We'll talk. Perhaps we can work something out."

Arnold turned around. Two steps later he felt the knife plunge through his flesh and slit through the veins in his neck. Blood gushed from everywhere. Images of his wife and daughter flashed though his mind and then dissolved into total blackness.

It was ten past three in the afternoon when Damien and Durk recieved word that Arnold Sawyer, a senior agent with twenty-plus years of service and a spotless record, had been murdered in his office. He had been one of the key players in the failed operations and searches of Enmascardo Island. Caudillo knew how to pick his sources.

"So that's it," Durk said. "A dead agent can't talk."

"So much for my plan," Damien said.

"It wasn't your fault it failed or that Agent Sawyer is dead."

"Somehow that doesn't make me feel any better." He walked over to the counter and poured himself another cup of strong black coffee. He carried it back to the kitchen table. The waiting for Caudillo to appear at the ranch was starting to grate big-time on his nerves.

"It's so quiet around here that it's almost eerie," Damien said.

"I was just thinking the same thing. If Caudillo is coming, I hope he makes it soon."

But he didn't make it soon. Afternoon turned to the hazy shadows of twilight and then the full blackness of a cloudy, starless night shrouded the ranch.

Finally, Durk sacked out on the couch while Damien added another log to the fireplace.

"If I fall asleep, wake me at the first hint of trouble," Durk said.

"I will." The first streaks of sun were coming up over the horizon and filtering through the windows when Damien finally closed his eyes. When he did, it was as if a curtain opened and Emma appeared on the stage. Only she wasn't alone.

A hideous monster was there with her, pulling her into his lap, running his fingers through her silky hair. Brushing her flesh with hands that looked like claws.

"You can't save her," the monster cried. "You're not a Lambert."

The voice belonged to his father.

Damien jerked awake. His heart was pounding. Bright sunshine flooded the room. His phone was jangling loudly. He jumped from the chair where he'd fallen asleep and took the call, praying that Caudillo had arrived at Bent

Pine Ranch and was already in the clutches of the CIA. "Damien here," he answered.

"This is Jerry Delaney. I have news."

"Good, I hope."

"The best. You can stop worrying about Caudillo or Anton Klein as we know him."

"Does that mean you have him in custody?"

"No. It means he's dead. It seems he wasn't in the United States when he called the ranch."

As much as he'd like to, Damien couldn't quite accept that it was over. "How do you know this?"

"There was an explosion on his yacht this afternoon at about the same time someone was slitting Sawyer's throat. Five crewmen are missing, supposedly thrown into the water by the force of the blast. But not Caudillo's. His body was found on board and identified by the captain."

"So all you have is the captain's word?"

"No. The boat is in port and the the local authorities did a fingerprint check. There's an exact match. And now I have someone here who'd like to say hello."

"It's over, Damien. It's really over. The monster is dead."

Emma's voice sang with excitement. "I'm on my way back to the ranch and I can't wait to see you."

"I'll be here." He wanted to say so much more. Like the fact that he loved her. That he never wanted her out of his life. But words could wait. Emma was safe and she was coming back to him.

EMMA COULDN'T STOP SMILING. It was as if her heart were so full of happiness that it might burst from her chest.

She knew she'd still have nightmares about her time with Caudillo. There would still be days when she'd wake up and for a horrifying second think she was still locked away in his island fortress. But those times would grow fewer and further apart. She'd never forget the horrors, but she wouldn't let them rob her of her happiness, either.

Damien was waiting outside when the car she was in pulled up in front of the rambling ranch house. She jumped from the car and into his arms. He swung her around as if she were a kid, making her dizzy with excitement and desire. And then he pulled her to him and held her so close she could barely breathe.

When his lips met hers, she melted into his kiss. She could have stayed in his arms forever had not the rest of the family rushed out to welcome her home.

Minutes later, they'd all gathered on the glassed-in porch and the celebration shifted into high gear. Tague popped the cork on the champagne. Emma settled into the rocker, cradling the precious Belle in her arms while life, laughter and intoxicating relief rocked the room.

Carolina pulled a chair up next to Emma. "I have a confession to make."

"Confess anything today and I'd forgive you."

"I was a nervous wreck last night, and I just kept thinking I had to do something positive. I hope you don't consider this meddling in your affairs, but I called around and found out that the daughter of a friend of mine is one of the supervisors in charge of finding foster parents in our area. So I called her and explained the situation with Belle."

Emma held her breath, not sure she wanted to hear the rest of this confession. "What did you find out?"

"That there's a real shortage of foster homes for infants in this area. She sees no reason why they can't place Belle in your care until the father is located if you'll take the fostering-parent classes and if you're approved as a foster parent. I'm sure you will be."

"Me? Keep Belle?"

"Only if you want to. And if you agree to stay in the county. But it will still only be until they find the real father."

Emma's eyes filled with tears. "I don't know what to say. I *so* want to take care of Belle as long as she needs me. And when I have to give her up, I'll just have to handle it. Thanks. Thank you for everything."

"It's partly selfish, you know. I'm not ready to lose either of you."

And if Damien loved her as much as she did him, Carolina would get her wish. But as yet, Damien had not mentioned love. Maybe it was only the fact that she needed protection that had turned him on.

No, she didn't believe that. He might not have said the words yet, but she'd seen love in his eyes and felt it in his touch.

Yet when she looked for him she realized that he'd slipped away from the celebration and was nowhere in sight.

CAROLINA SLIPPED OUT THE back door and followed Damien as he took the well-worn path to the horse barn. The letter she'd cherished for years was clutched in her right hand. Running, she caught up with Damien and slipped her left arm though his. "It's not like you to leave a family celebration."

"That was when I thought I knew where I fit in the family."

"I was afraid that might be behind your swift mood change."

"You should have told me sooner that I was adopted."

"I know that now, but you were too young at first. By the time you were old enough, it didn't seem worth the argument it would have caused with Hugh. Besides, you were always our son in our hearts. To tell you the truth, I don't see how you can't know that."

"Did you insist Dad leave the house to me?"

"The subject never came up, Damien. You were the firstborn. The house was rightfully yours. Look, I know you had issues with Hugh at times. He was hard on you, but he loved you. I know telling you that isn't getting through to you, but perhaps this will." She handed him the letter and then turned and walked back to the house, leaving him to read it in privacy.

DAMIEN LEANED ON THE DOOR to the tack room as he read the letter.

> Happy First Anniversary to my beautiful and dearly beloved wife.

Damien felt like an intruder as he read the proclamations of love written to his mother. It wasn't until the last paragraphs that he realized why she'd given him the letter to read.

> I'm still awed by the miracle of our son, Damien. You brought me love and a zest for life. Damien has brought me a reason to be an example of all that a man should be. I expected to love him. I never expected him to become the center of our life and for me to enjoy just watching and playing with him so much.
>
> I just pray that we have a houseful of more sons and that we'll love them just as much—if that's even possible.

Damien reread the letter, more slowly this time, letting the words sink in. The fierce sense of betrayal faded a bit. Maybe he had overreacted and judged his father falsely. It would take time to work that out in his mind. But even he couldn't deny that being a part of the Lambert family was embedded in his very soul.

He pushed the thoughts aside to deal with on another day. Right now, he had to make a few urgent decisions on how to ask Emma to be his wife, and he always thought better on horseback. He didn't want to rush her. He'd give her all the time she needed.

God help him if it took too long. How many cold showers could he survive?

An hour later, Damien still hadn't returned to the house. When Belle began to fret, Emma pulled a light blanket around her and walked into the backyard to soak up some sunshine. The cold spell had passed and the January temperature was flirting with the seventy-degree mark.

She walked to the swing and sat down, moving her feet just enough to create the gentle swaying movement that soothed Belle when nothing else could.

"You're my miracle, Belle. If not for you, I would have never stayed on this ranch long enough to fall in love with Damien."

She heard frootsteps behind her and spun around.

"So you love him? Isn't that nice?"

Caudillo. Only this time the voice was more than a nightmare in her head.

She opened her mouth to scream, but Caudillo's left hand closed over her lips. His right one pushed the tip of a knife between her shoulder blades and plunged it into her flesh. Hot, sticky blood ran down her back.

"Scream and I'll kill the baby. You know I will, so don't

tempt me." This time he let the knife cut along her arm, and the blood dripped onto her shoe and into the dirt.

"Now get up and start walking away from the house toward that cluster of trees. Your rope is waiting, my dear."

Paralyzing fear ran ice-cold through her veins. "You're supposed to be dead."

"And you're supposed to be on Enmascarado Island."

The terrifying truth infiltrated her horror. "You weren't on that yacht when it blew up."

"Now, how did you guess?"

"But you planned that explosion. You killed your own crew."

"Everyone has to die sometime."

"How did you fake the fingerprints?"

"Silly girl. Silly, silly girl. Money buys anything a man wants. I'm sure your new boyfriend knows that. Damien Lambert is one of the richest men in Texas. But you like money and yachts. That's what attracted you to me."

"Damien is nothing like you, Caudillo. Nothing."

"I wouldn't be so sure of that, but it doesn't really matter. You won't live to find out. Now start walking." The point of the knife plunged into the flesh between her shoulder blades and she felt a hot, sticky trickle of blood slide down her back. She walked as if in a torturous trance.

"It didn't have to be this way, Emma. Of all the girls I chose, you are the one I might have cherished. And yet you were repulsed at my touch." He shoved her again and she stumbled forward and into the cluster of trees.

"Now lay the baby on the grass and take off those horrid clothes that a real woman would never be caught dead in." He chuckled at his own sick joke.

He was going to kill her. But not quickly. That wasn't his style. She remembered the story of the woman he'd tortured, cutting off her breasts and then—

No. She would not let him paralyze her with fear when she had to save herself. She was not ready to die.

"If you want my clothes off, you'll have to take them off yourself."

He pushed her to the ground and put the knife to Belle's chest. "Is this what you want?"

Her heart plunged to the depths of her soul. "No, don't hurt Belle. Please, Caudillo. I'll do anything you say, just don't hurt Belle."

She shed her clothes slowly. Only after she was naked did she look up and see the noose a few yards away, dangling from the branch of an oak tree. He'd torture her and then he'd hang her.

Damien would find her like that.

Caudillo always won.

Chapter Seventeen

Damien was dismounting when his cell phone rang. He started to ignore it, but then saw the call was from Carson Stile.

"I guess you're calling to tell me that Caudillo is dead," Damien said in lieu of a greeting.

"No, I'm calling to tell you he's in the Dallas area near your ranch."

"What makes you think that?"

"He used his ATM card to withdraw cash at that same hardware store where you talked me into buying those ridiculous spurs."

Damien tossed the phone and raced into the house.

"What's the rush?" Carolina asked when he crashed into her.

"Where's Emma?"

"She took Belle outside. What's wrong?"

"Outside where?"

"In the back. The last time I saw her she was walking toward that old tire swing."

"Where are Tague and Durk?"

"They left in Tague's pickup truck."

"Stay in the house and lock the doors. And call Tague and Durk and tell them to get home on the double. I think Caudillo is heading this way."

"I thought it was over," Carolina cried. "I thought he was dead."

Damien didn't even think about stopping to explain. He grabbed the pistol that he'd kept handy last night and ran to find Emma.

Instead he found blood. Drops of it beneath the swing like crimson raindrops in the dirt. Oh, God, don't let him be too late. If he'd let something happen to Emma…

Dread and adrenaline pushed him on, slowly, quietly, moving from tree to tree so he wouldn't be seen.

And then he spotted Emma through the trees. She was naked, her hands and feet bound, her neck in a noose. Her feet were still on the ground, but the loose end of the rope was in Caudillo's hand. One yank and her neck would break.

Belle was lying on the grass, eyes closed, not moving. Sick terror ground in Damien's gut.

"If you kill me, Damien will track you to the ends of the world and make you pay."

"Do you honestly think I'm afraid of a cowboy?"

Damien had never killed a man before, yet he relished the idea of putting a bullet in Caudillo's head.

And the way he saw it, Caudillo gave him no other choice. One yank of the rope and Emma was dead, and he had no doubt that if Caudillo saw him, he'd make sure Emma's neck was broken.

Damien would have one shot. He'd have to make it count. He fit his finger around the trigger, held steady and pulled.

EMMA HEARD THE BLAST OF gunfire and thought for a second it was the crack of death. Belle's screams jerked her back to reality.

Caudillo lay on the ground in a pool of blood.

Damien rushed over, took the noose from her neck and pulled her into his arms. "Are you okay? Did he hurt you?"

"No, he was just getting warmed up. It's the mental game he loved." She began to shake. "Is he dead?"

"He's dead. Even Caudillo can't live with his brain splattered across Bent Pine grass."

He yanked off his shirt and wrapped it around her. "I have never been that afraid in all my life. I don't ever want to be that afraid again."

"Apparently neither does Belle." She hurried over to pick up the screaming baby. Belle hushed almost immediately. She handed the baby off to Damien while she slipped back into her jeans.

He put his arm around Emma and pulled her back into the shelter of his embrace.

"I'm crazy in love with you, Emma. I don't know how I fell so hard and so fast, but I'm there."

"I feel the same, Damien. I think I loved you since you found me in the snow. Like your dad and mother, we were meant to be."

"Does that mean you'll marry me?"

"In a heartbeat."

Emma looked up as Tague and Durk came running through the trees.

"What the hell is going on? Mother yelled at me to get home fast and then I hear— Whoa." Durk stopped and stared at the body.

"Is that who I think it is?"

"That's the monster," Emma said. "He wasn't dead, but he is now. Your brother just saved my life."

"What happened?"

"I'll fill you in later," Damien told him. "Right now, call the sheriff. Tell him we have another self-defense killing at the Bent Pine Ranch."

"I'll call Delaney, too," Durk said. "He's going to have a devil of a time getting his head around this."

"Are you and Belle both okay?" Tague asked.

"Better than okay. We're alive," Emma said.

She fit Belle against her right shoulder as Damien wrapped an arm about her waist.

"Let's go home, cowboy." Home to stay.

Carolina was right. A woman should always choose love.

* * * * *

SUSPENSE

Harlequin

INTRIGUE®

COMING NEXT MONTH
AVAILABLE MAY 8, 2012

#1347 COLBY LAW
Colby, TX
Debra Webb

#1348 SECRET AGENDA
Cooper Security
Paula Graves

#1349 OBSESSION
Guardians of Coral Cove
Carol Ericson

#1350 THE MARINE NEXT DOOR
The Precinct: Task Force
Julie Miller

#1351 PRIVATE SECURITY
The Delancey Dynasty
Mallory Kane

#1352 WHEN SHE WASN'T LOOKING
HelenKay Dimon

You can find more information on upcoming Harlequin®
titles, free excerpts and more at www.Harlequin.com.

HICNM0412

REQUEST YOUR FREE BOOKS!
2 FREE NOVELS PLUS 2 FREE GIFTS!

Harlequin®

INTRIGUE®

BREATHTAKING ROMANTIC SUSPENSE

YES! Please send me 2 FREE Harlequin Intrigue® novels and my 2 FREE gifts (gifts are worth about $10). After receiving them, if I don't wish to receive any more books, I can return the shipping statement marked "cancel." If I don't cancel, I will receive 6 brand-new novels every month and be billed just $4.49 per book in the U.S. or $5.24 per book in Canada. That's a saving of at least 14% off the cover price! It's quite a bargain! Shipping and handling is just 50¢ per book in the U.S. and 75¢ per book in Canada.* I understand that accepting the 2 free books and gifts places me under no obligation to buy anything. I can always return a shipment and cancel at any time. Even if I never buy another book, the two free books and gifts are mine to keep forever.

182/382 HDN FEQ2

Name _____ (PLEASE PRINT)

Address _____ Apt. #

City _____ State/Prov. _____ Zip/Postal Code

Signature (if under 18, a parent or guardian must sign)

Mail to the Reader Service:
IN U.S.A.: P.O. Box 1867, Buffalo, NY 14240-1867
IN CANADA: P.O. Box 609, Fort Erie, Ontario L2A 5X3

Not valid for current subscribers to Harlequin Intrigue books.

**Are you a subscriber to Harlequin Intrigue books
and want to receive the larger-print edition?
Call 1-800-873-8635 or visit www.ReaderService.com.**

* Terms and prices subject to change without notice. Prices do not include applicable taxes. Sales tax applicable in N.Y. Canadian residents will be charged applicable taxes. Offer not valid in Quebec. This offer is limited to one order per household. All orders subject to credit approval. Credit or debit balances in a customer's account(s) may be offset by any other outstanding balance owed by or to the customer. Please allow 4 to 6 weeks for delivery. Offer available while quantities last.

Your Privacy—The Reader Service is committed to protecting your privacy. Our Privacy Policy is available online at www.ReaderService.com or upon request from the Reader Service.

We make a portion of our mailing list available to reputable third parties that offer products we believe may interest you. If you prefer that we not exchange your name with third parties, or if you wish to clarify or modify your communication preferences, please visit us at www.ReaderService.com/consumerchoice or write to us at Reader Service Preference Service, P.O. Box 9062, Buffalo, NY 14269. Include your complete name and address.

HI11B

Colby Investigator Lyle McCaleb is on the case.
But can he protect Sadie Gilmore from her haunting past?

Harlequin Intrigue® presents a new installment
in Debra Webb's miniseries, COLBY, TX.

Enjoy a sneak peek of COLBY LAW.

With the shotgun hanging at her side, she made it as far as
the porch steps, when the driver's side door opened. Sadie
knew the deputies in Coryell County. Her visitor wasn't any
of them. A boot hit the ground, stirring the dust. Something deep inside her braced for a new kind of trouble.
As the driver emerged, Sadie's gaze moved upward, over
the gleaming black door and the tinted window to a black
Stetson and dark sunglasses. She couldn't quite make out
the details of the man's face but some extra sense that had
nothing to do with what she could see set her on edge.

Another boot hit the ground and the door closed. Her
visual inspection swept over long legs cinched in comfort-
ably worn denim, a lean waist and broad shoulders testing
the seams of a shirt that hadn't come off the rack at any
store where she shopped, finally zeroing in on the man's
face just as he removed the dark glasses.

The weapon almost slipped from her grasp. Her heart
bucked hard twice, then skidded to a near halt.

Lyle McCaleb.

"What the…devil?" whispered past her lips.

Unable to move a muscle, she watched in morbid fasci-
nation as he hooked the sunglasses on to his hip pocket and
strode toward the house—toward her. Sadie wouldn't have
been able to summon a warning that he was trespassing had
her life depended on it.

Lyle glanced at the shotgun as he reached up and removed his hat. "Expecting company?"

As if her heart had suddenly started to pump once more, kicking her brain into gear, fury blasted through her frozen muscles. "What do you want, Lyle McCaleb?"

"Seeing as you didn't know I was coming, that couldn't be for me." He gave a nod toward her shotgun.

This could not be happening. Seven years he'd been gone. This was…this was… "I have nothing to say to you." She turned her back to him and walked away. Who did he think he was, showing up here like this after all this time? It was crazy. He was crazy!

"I know I'm the last person on this earth you want to see."

Her feet stopped when she wanted to keep going. To get inside the house and slam the door and dead bolt it.

"We need to talk."

The stakes are high as Lyle fights for the woman he loves. But can he solve the case in time to save an innocent life?

Find out in COLBY LAW
Available May 2012 from Harlequin Intrigue®
wherever books are sold.